Raoul was a

Emma felt a searing pain deep in her chest, and she suddenly found breathing difficult. How long had he been a monk? Why had he waited until the day of their wedding to turn his back on her forever?

Unable to stand the suspense a moment longer, she called out to him. "Father John!"

He straightened to his full height with an abruptness that told Emma she'd caught him off guard. "Madam?" He spoke warily. His back was to the light, his tall frame merely a dark shape.

She started to shiver. "Raoul?" she whispered. "I—it's Emma."

She heard his sharp intake of breath, saw the way he seemed, ever so briefly, to stagger at the revelation. "So it *was* you...."

DEAR READER:

The Colorado Rockies, the setting for this story, is one of the most exciting—and romantic!—places on earth. If you've never been there, especially in winter, I hope *Rescued Heart* will give you an idea of what that experience is like.

The Mount of the Holy Cross, over fourteen thousand feet in elevation, is located in the Sawatch Range near Vail, Colorado, and does, indeed, exist. It's not only the site of a long-abandoned mining town, but was at one time a national symbol of Christian faith and the destination of several pilgrimages, due to the natural formation of a cross on the side of the mountain.

Though the Abbey of the Holy Cross is pure fabrication, it *could* exist, as there is a Trappist monastery located at the popular nearby ski resort of Snowmass, Colorado. The monks manufacture gourmet cookies as a means of livelihood, and provide assistance for those in need.

I hope you'll enjoy Emma and Raoul's love story. It's a story I've wanted to write for years; one that still haunts my dreams.

REBECCA WINTERS

RESCUED HEART

Rebecca Winters

Harlequin Books

TORONTO • NEW YORK • LONDON
AMSTERDAM • PARIS • SYDNEY • HAMBURG
STOCKHOLM • ATHENS • TOKYO • MILAN

ISBN 0-373-03162-9

Harlequin Romance first edition November 1991

RESCUED HEART

Printed in U.S.A.

CHAPTER ONE

SNOW FLURRIES GAVE WAY to blizzard conditions as the Wagoneer left the alpine meadows and followed the winding road through Colorado's Sawatch mountain range.

To Emma Wakefield, the peaks loomed like giant sentinels. The sun had gone down behind the one called Notch Mountain, and the heavy cloud cover made five o'clock in the afternoon feel like nine at night.

Stephen Channing let out a low whistle. "How would you have liked being one of the seventeenth-century Spanish explorers, wading through these drifts without the benefit of a heater?"

"Perish the thought," Emma said, grimacing. She fed him another morsel of mint-chocolate truffle while he concentrated on his driving. They'd long since passed the permanent snow line. Her thoughts went to the Saint Bernard slumbering in the rear of the van. The rare disease that had affected the dog's eyes was in remission and they were returning her to the kennel in the mountains. "Knowing we have Dame Margaret with us makes me feel secure."

"My darling girl," Stephen began, his warm blue eyes twinkling as they rested briefly on Emma, "are you intimating that you don't think I'm capable of keeping you warm?"

A teasing smile lifted the corner of her full mouth. Stephen was tall and large-boned, with an open, gentle spirit. Both Emma and her sister, Lorna, had often likened Stephen to the adorable Saint Bernards, huge but harmless and possessing delightful dispositions. "Between the two of you, I'm not the least worried."

He chuckled. "We're almost at the monastery. I'm sorry you're not going to see the abbey clearly. I might have known we'd arrive in the middle of a storm. Over the last ten years I've made this trip dozens of times, but I've never seen the weather this ferocious in November."

Emma kept silent. At one time she'd been an excellent skier and had fallen deeply in love with a French-Canadian mountaineering expert, but Stephen didn't know that. And he didn't know she'd planned to move to Quebec; she had even begun learning French. All she'd ever told Stephen was that the man she'd planned to marry two years earlier had mysteriously disappeared before the ceremony. Her loss had been so devastating she'd never been able to share the details with anyone outside her immediate family.

Since then, she hadn't gone near a ski resort. Winter had come to represent something almost too painful to endure. Only the demands of her career as a veterinarian could make her venture this far from Denver. Being in the mountains now took her fleeting back to a period in her life when she'd known intense joy.

By the time they'd passed the last ski area at the ten-thousand-foot level, she regretted the decision to accompany Stephen, even though her duties as a vet included servicing the kennel in the mountains.

Memories of another life pressed in on her until she felt suffocated. Without being aware of it, she gripped the edge of the seat.

Stephen darted her a concerned glance. "A few more minutes, Emma. One more bend in the road and then we can relax. Don't be nervous."

Emma didn't bother to correct him. So much the better if he thought her tension stemmed from fear of the elements. Once they'd delivered Dame Margaret to the abbey's kennel, Emma felt sure she'd be all right. Her work helped keep unwanted, unbidden thoughts at bay.

After they'd given routine vaccinations and examined one of the dogs suspected of having hip dysplasia, she and Stephen would head home, then spend the rest of the week in Puerto Vallarta, Mexico, getting a suntan. It couldn't come soon enough for Emma.

"Hang on!" Stephen shouted as he negotiated a curve on the treacherous, narrow mountain road. A strong gust of wind screamed through the top of Half Moon Pass, hitting the van broadside. "We're sliding off the road!"

Everything happened so quickly Emma didn't have a chance to cry out. The Wagoneer careered to the left and came to rest in a snowdrift. There was a crunch of metal on her side, and then all went quiet.

"Emma? Are you all right?" Stephen called out anxiously.

"I'm fine," she answered in a shaky voice. "Truly. The damage is on the outside of the door. How are you?"

"Forget me!" He reached over, unfastened her seat belt and pulled her against him. "I can't believe what happened."

"It was a freak accident," she said, attempting to reassure him. "Stop worrying about it. I can get out your side."

He hugged her long and hard, despite the obstacle presented by the steering wheel. "The abbey isn't more than a couple of hundred yards from here. I'll go for help. If you want to come with me, I won't stop you, but you'll be warmer if you stay inside. Emma, I'm sorry." He sighed deeply, his breath fanning her curly, golden hair. "That last gust of wind was a killer. I couldn't steer."

"No one could have done better. We didn't even overturn." She'd never seen Stephen this vulnerable, and it brought out her protective instincts. "I'm grateful we've come out of this with nothing more than a few dents. Dame Margaret's still asleep, so stop blaming yourself."

"I'd better go for help. Will you be nervous here alone?"

"With Dame Margaret for company? Are you joking?" She laughed. "We'll both be fine."

"Right," he muttered, releasing her to make his way to the area behind their seats where they'd placed the luggage and their ski equipment. He switched on the heavy-duty flashlight and shone it at Dame Margaret's cage. "She's dead to the world. Probably won't wake up until tomorrow morning. She could keep you warm, Emma, but that's about all."

"Will you stop it?" Touched by his concern, she tried to sound lighthearted. Still, the howling of the wind seemed to be intensifying. They were surrounded by a white, alien world. She couldn't repress a horrified shudder at the far more serious accident that might have happened. In this isolated place, with these conditions, no one would know, perhaps for days, that they'd gone off the road.

The tracks made by the tires were already covered by fresh snow. She shivered again, despite the warmth of the van as her fears for Stephen's safety increased. "Please be careful! You can wander around in circles during a storm like this."

"I'm not a Boy Scout leader for nothing," he told her, pulling on a pair of insulated gloves. His comment brought a faint smile to Emma's lips. Though divorced, he managed to spend considerable time with his two sons, camping and fishing. She knew he was a competent woodsman. Stephen was the kind of man who brought a full commitment to everything he did, especially if it concerned his profession or his family. Emma had nothing but admiration for him.

"I'm ready now, and I'll be back with help inside fifteen minutes." As he eased his big body to the door of the van, he leaned over the seat and brushed her cheek with his lips. "For luck," he murmured.

When he'd gone, she gently touched the place where his lips had lingered. It was the first time he'd taken that kind of liberty. Six months ago, Stephen had hired her fresh from veterinary school. He needed her expertise with large breeds to fill a vacancy at his clinic in Denver. Since then, he'd frequently taken her out to dinner and various events; he made no secret of the fact that he wanted a permanent relationship with her.

Perhaps in time she could learn to love him. An ache passed through her body at the idea of spending the rest of her life alone. If she reached out to him on this trip, maybe the pain of Raoul's disappearance would leave once and for all. She owed it to both of them to try.

Stephen had been through the agony of divorce, but he didn't seem afraid to embrace life again. That was what she had to do. Embrace life! Lorna had urged her to spend this week with Stephen for her own good.

Emma watched Stephen's progress until the light looked like a firefly in the distance. When it vanished, she took a deep breath and rested her head against the back of the seat.

Because of the way the Wagoneer had tilted, she propped her feet against the gearshift to keep from sliding to the left. After a few minutes, she got another truffle from her bag and slowly ate it.

She couldn't help recalling the conversation she and Stephen had had the day he'd proposed the trip. "Don't you think two years is long enough to mourn an event that wasn't meant to be?" he'd asked her. "Love has to be fed. You've been living on memories—not the real thing."

Sighing, Emma switched off the ignition. The interior of the van had grown too warm. Her ski sweater and bibs would protect her from the cold for a while. She hadn't worn these clothes for more than two years. They represented another lifetime...another age. That was how she felt, that she'd come from another age, another planet, all enthusiasm for life gone out of her.

Without conscious volition, Emma once again began to relive those moments with Raoul at the airport before he'd flown home to Montreal to prepare for the wedding. Not wanting to be separated from him even for a minute, Emma had clung to him as he embraced her one more time before getting out of the car. They'd agreed to say their goodbyes in private, rather than inside the terminal.

"Darling," she'd cried in a low, husky voice, throwing her arms about his bronzed neck. "I'm going to miss you so much," she murmured against his lips. Crushing her to his chest, he buried his face in her freshly washed hair and inhaled the scent.

"Do you think I want to leave?" he'd whispered before kissing her once more. "Another week, Emma, and then I'm never letting you out of my sight again."

She remembered how the tears had trickled down her cheeks, surprising Raoul. "Darling? What's wrong?"

She'd held him tighter. "I can't stand any more separations. There've been too many of them."

Raoul had grasped her hands and kissed the palms. "This will be the last one, I swear." And she knew he meant it.

"You'll phone me tonight?" she'd asked, voice breaking, as he got out of her car.

"Can you doubt it?" He'd leaned through the open window and cupped her face in his hands, kissing her thoroughly. But Emma had difficulty letting him go. She couldn't explain the sudden panic that possessed her.

"Don't let anything happen to you. I plan to become Mrs. Raoul Villard a week from today. I don't know if I can wait that long!"

"Emma..." Raoul had pressed a hard kiss on her mouth, then turned away abruptly. She'd watched him stride across the tarmac, and it was as though he'd taken her heart with him. His black hair and tall lean body caught the attention of several people. Emma stared until he disappeared into the throng.

True to his promise, he called her daily until her own departure for Canada. There were last-minute plans to make for the ceremony and the subsequent wedding receptions being held in Montreal and Denver. Not only that, they had to make arrangements to ship Emma's belongings to Montreal. They'd be living there after the wedding. Since his days of ski instructing were over, Raoul had planned to join his family's exporting business. As for Emma, her plans were to complete her veterinary studies in Quebec. After the honeymoon...

On *that* particular subject, Raoul remained mysteriously silent. She had no idea where they were going—and didn't particularly care. All that mattered was having him to herself; after a courtship punctuated with drives to and from the airport and long waits in between while Raoul went off to ski workshops. For the first time, it would be just the two of them, hidden away from the demands and distractions of the world. But then fate had stepped in to dash her dreams to pieces.

A sudden low moan made Emma jump. She looked over her shoulder. Dame Margaret could be waking up, but Emma had a hunch the dog was dreaming. She listened, but heard no more sounds. The magnificent animal slept on, oblivious to their dilemma.

The high altitude made Emma sleepy, too. She closed her eyes and rested her head between the seat and the window, trying to find a comfortable position for her long legs.

Dear Stephen. He was doing everything in his power not only to make this a memorable trip but to deepen his relationship with her. Yet images of Raoul's darkly handsome face filled her mind—her heart—to the exclusion of all else. He'd loved these mountains. Being here again had brought him so forcefully to mind that Emma had to swallow back a sob of despair. Maybe she was the kind of woman destined to love only one man.

Some of Emma's friends were already working on their second marriages. They didn't seem to have any difficulty loving more than one person. What was wrong with her?

A tapping against the window jarred her from her painful thoughts. "Emma?" As Stephen opened the door, enormous snowflakes blew into the van on a howling gust of wind. She felt its bite through to her bones as Stephen reached for her.

"Did you think I was never coming?" His question left her feeling vaguely guilty, since her mind had been on the man she was here to forget, not on Stephen or their imminent rescue. "Two monks from the abbey brought me back in a Jeep. One of them'll run you up to the abbey while the other helps me with Dame Margaret."

"That's wonderful." She put on her parka. "What about the Wagoneer?" After slipping on her ski gloves, she drew a knitted wool hat down over her forehead and ears.

"They'll go back for chains to pull it from the snowbank in a few minutes. When I've got the dog settled in the kennel, I'll join you."

With Stephen's steadying hand on her elbow, she jumped to the ground and found herself knee-deep in fresh powder. Overbalancing, she fell against him. "Oh, I'm sorry."

He gave her a squeeze. "I'm not. To tell you the truth, I've wanted to feel you in my arms like this for a long time." The yearning in his voice didn't go undetected by Emma as he assisted her up the slope, making her feel worse than ever because her thoughts had been centered on Raoul.

She hated herself for what she was doing to Stephen. Any other woman would consider herself the luckiest person in the world to be loved by him! Emma was being given a second chance and she'd better grab it. Squaring her shoulders as she squinted against the blowing snow, she determined once and for all to enjoy this trip with Stephen and to return his feelings if she possibly could.

The wind grew bolder once they reached the main road where the Jeep stood. She could just discern the silhouette of a figure in the driver's seat. The other monk raised a gloved hand in a gesture of acknowledgment, then made his way down to the Wagoneer in a few agile movements. The snow meant poor visibility, and she shivered again. What if they'd been stranded without help?

"Up you go," Stephen murmured, opening the door to assist her into the back of the Jeep. "I'll see you in a few minutes." To Emma's surprise, he climbed inside after her, kissing her softly, this time on her unsuspecting mouth. Her first instinct was to draw away from the contact, but she forced herself to respond and discovered that it was rather enjoyable.

"Did I just dream you kissed me back?" he whispered in awe. He sounded so happy she found she wanted him to stay like that.

"No," she said after a moment's hesitation. "Actually, I'm glad you talked me into coming with you, after all." And it was true. Raoul belonged to the past. Today she was closing the door on his memory.

"Will wonders never cease?" The silly grin made her laugh out loud. "I'll join you soon." He jumped out of the Jeep and shut the door.

"If you're ready, madam." The voice of the monk at the wheel was deep, masculine.

"Of course." She blinked as he turned the vehicle around and headed up the mountain road. Color stained Emma's cheeks as she bowed her head, embarrassed. A man who'd taken vows of celibacy probably found her byplay with Stephen trifling. At least, the slight hint of mockery in the man's tone led her to think that.

Then again, it was probably her imagination. For two years Emma's emotions had been encased in ice and only now was she attempting to break free, for Stephen's sake.

She stared out the side window. The snow wasn't coming down quite as hard as before. Suddenly she caught a glimpse of the gray stone structure of the monastery. Partially buried in snow, it stood near the base of one of the most notable mountains in America, Mount of the Holy Cross, from which the abbey derived its name.

The peak rose to a majestic fourteen thousand feet. The huge white cross on its northeast face gave the site an air of quiet mystery. Emma had read that there was a snow formation to the right of the cross known as the Supplicating Virgin, and that the lake at the base was named the Bowl of Tears.

Before she left the abbey, Emma hoped to see the legendary geological formation that in earlier times had been a national symbol of Christian faith.

Stephen explained that they'd be staying in guest rooms at the abbey. The kennel was situated beneath the building for easy access, since the monks made their living breeding, training and selling Saint Bernards.

Emma gazed delightedly at the majestic nineteenth-century building, enjoying the contrast between its solid warmth and the starkness surrounding it. The Jeep stopped suddenly and her attention swung to the driver. As he turned to face her, his hood fell away, revealing short, jet-black hair with an obvious natural tendency to curl. Emma stared at his strong neck, burnished to a deep mahogany by the high-altitude sun.

The breath caught in her throat as a feeling of déjà
vu swept over her. Had her sick preoccupation with
the past brought her to the point that she imagined
every fit man with black hair and suntanned skin to be
Raoul? Even this priest? Her obsession with Raoul's
memory had to stop!

He pushed down the bucket seat to help her climb
out of the Jeep, but Emma's eyes fastened helplessly
on the broad shoulders covered by a dark gray parka.
Straight as a lance, the priest conveyed the energy and
power of a man in his prime. Emma sat there trans-
fixed. Perhaps the accident had affected her more
deeply than she'd thought. Was her mind playing
tricks on her?

Like Raoul, who could ski before he could walk, the
priests of the abbey were at home in the mountains.
Raoul had been invited to demonstrate survival tech-
niques at a special ski workshop in Vail, where Emma
had first met him. These priests, too, were skilled in
the lifesaving procedures so often needed in the frozen wilderness of the Rockies.

Every year there were accidents like the one she and
Stephen had experienced. He'd told her how many
rescues the monks had been responsible for last year;
she couldn't remember the number. Stephen loved
facts and figures, she thought fondly. He always said
her more intuitive approach complemented his perfectly. She'd be a fool to allow Raoul's memory to destroy this chance for a real relationship with Stephen.
Still . . .

As she jumped down, the dim light from the vehicle's interior revealed a bearded jaw and aquiline profile. It was only seconds, but like the relief on a coin, the rugged slant of hard cheekbone, straight nose and black slash of brow came into prominence. Long ago those exact physical traits had belonged to Raoul! Emma let out an involuntary cry as the world began to reel.

"May I be of assistance?" When the dizziness receded, Emma opened her eyes to discover she was being supported by a bearded priest in a belted white habit, who gazed at her with concern. His face was heavy-featured and weathered. "I'm Father André. You're suffering shock from your mishap. Father John felt you were in some distress. The high altitude has probably affected you, as well. You must have time to acclimatize, coming from Denver."

Emma moistened her lips. "I'm all right now," she murmured. Her eyes made a frantic search of the immediate area, but she saw no sign of the Jeep or the other priest, and she pressed a gloved hand to her throat. Evidently she'd lived with Raoul's image too long, and she'd started endowing any man faintly resembling him with his dark, commanding looks. She'd only had a glimpse of the priest's profile, but the resemblance seemed so uncanny.

"You say it was a Father John who brought me here?" The old priest nodded. "I'd like to thank him for helping me," she said, grasping his wiry hand so

she'd remain upright. He cupped her elbow securely
as she walked unsteadily through the deep snow.

"He's gone to get chains for the van, but I'll con-
vey your message of gratitude. Follow me."

They had reached massive wooden doors that
opened into a vaulted vestibule. Emma fixed her gaze
on the older priest, who moved with surprising agility
for his age.

"Sit down, please." He indicated a wooden bench
against the wall. "Drink this." He approached her
with a small snifter of brandy.

The strong vapors tickled her nose, but she did as he
said. He'd spoken the truth. She'd suffered a tremen-
dous shock just now. Though Emma didn't like the
taste of liquor, she drank all of it and felt its fiery
warmth travel down her throat. "Thank you, Father." She handed him the empty snifter.

His smile was gentle and reassuring. "Now I can say
welcome to the Abbey of the Holy Cross. We had no
idea you'd gone off the road until Dr. Channing suddenly appeared. One of our community will see to
your vehicle and get it to Minturn for repairs."

"You're very kind," she murmured. "When we left
Denver this morning, I didn't expect to be the object
of a rescue operation. I'm sorry if we've caused you
any inconvenience."

"Dr. Channing is an honored friend of the abbey.
We're happy to repay him for his services to our kennel. He says Dame Margaret wasn't injured."

"No," Emma said. "Only the Wagoneer suffered damage. She was sleeping soundly when I left her a few minutes ago."

"I'm happy to hear it. When he said there was another passenger, I thought of course he meant Dr. Holms."

Since coming to work for Stephen, she'd heard that remark a hundred times if she'd heard it once. "I'm sorry to tell you that Dr. Holms died in an accident. I was hired to replace him. Dr. Channing felt this was the perfect opportunity to introduce me to your kennel, since the large breeds are my specialty."

"Of course." His dark eyes looked thoughtful. Was Father André wondering why Stephen hadn't mentioned that he planned to bring a female colleague? Yet he didn't seem particularly discomfited. "As you know," he said equably enough, "our Saint Bernards are unique."

"Yes. I understand you've been mating your dogs with the short-haired strain from the Barry line in Switzerland."

"Yes, and it has produced a superior animal."

"I agree. Dame Margaret is magnificent. You know, Father, each time a new litter of pups is born, I marvel. They're remarkable animals. I owned a Saint Bernard until last year." Her voice quavered. Gertrude's death, immediately after her father's, had sent Emma into shock. She hadn't been able to think about getting a new dog. Except for Lorna and Donald, her

husband, who lived in Denver, Emma had lost everyone who'd ever mattered to her.

The priest nodded. "The dogs serve as our children." Then with a wink, he added, "But don't tell the
others I said so."

She gave him a smile. "It's a privilege to be here,
Father."

"The color is coming back to your cheeks. If you'll
follow me, I'll show you to your room. Dinner will be
served in the refectory when you're ready."

Emma trailed after the priest, awestruck by her
surroundings. The stone walls swallowed sound, and
she felt as if she'd gone back to the Middle Ages. They
climbed a flight of stairs and proceeded down a corridor lined with paintings. The haunting thought came
to her that if a man wanted to escape from civilization, this would be the place.

Father André indicated a bathroom on her left, then
opened one of the guest-room doors. "Maybe you,
like Dr. Channing, are an avid student of history.
Perhaps after dinner you'd care to browse in the museum," he offered as he lighted a small oil lamp. "It's
full of memorabilia from the years before Holy Cross
City became a ghost town. There are some priceless
paintings done by the noted English artist, Thomas
Moran, as well as books dating back to the Spanish
explorers."

"I'd love to see it," Emma said, feigning enthusiasm. The priest was being gracious and could have no
idea of the chaotic state of her thoughts.

He smiled and turned to go. "Dr. Channing's room is next door. If you need assistance, come and find me in my office." He inclined his head as Emma thanked him, then left. She closed the door, leaning heavily against it. She needed some time alone and thanked providence Stephen hadn't been nearby when she'd had that dizzy spell.

Stephen was a perceptive man and would start asking a lot of questions—questions she didn't want to answer. Questions about Raoul. She hadn't been able to discuss the horror of his disappearance with anyone outside her family, and still couldn't speak about it.

Emma looked around her with interest. The room resembled a nun's cell; a bed, wardrobe and dresser with washbowl constituted its only furnishings. Her gaze wandered to the crucifix over the lintel. The stone walls ensured absolute quiet.

Throwing her hat and gloves on the bed, she walked over to the window. The storm that had caused their accident had blown itself out. She strained to detect movement outside, but all she could see was a blanket of snow below the jagged peaks, which rose like black phantoms above the abbey.

She pressed her forehead against the icy pane, unable to erase the encounter with Father John from her mind. If she could just see him again, face-to-face,

maybe she could lay these insane suspicions to rest.
Because, except for the beard, she'd stake her life on
the premise that Raoul was driving the Jeep. But the
very idea was ludicrous!

CHAPTER TWO

EMMA HID HER FACE in her hands. Raoul was gone, presumed dead. He'd never arrived at the church in Montreal where they were to be married.

She remembered every detail of that day....

Emma had entered the reception area of the church aided by her sister, Lorna, and their father. The floor-length, ivory peau-de-soie wedding gown rustled with each movement. Lorna held the train so it wouldn't trail on the ground.

The previous seven days had seemed like seven years, but the waiting had finally come to an end. The incessant knocking of her heart prevented Emma from achieving an outward calm. Her flushed cheeks needed no artifice.

"Relax, sweetheart," her father murmured, his blue eyes twinkling with a mixture of fatherly pride and concern. "It's the groom who's supposed to be nervous." He chuckled before brushing her hot cheek with his lips. "People will accuse me of being biased, but you're a vision to behold. I'd like to think your mother is looking on."

Tears sprang to her eyes. "I love you, Daddy. Thank you for putting up with me this past week. I know I've been impossible, but the constant separations from Raoul have been hard on both of us." Her eyes darted around the room. "I wish he'd hurry and get here."

Emma's father squeezed her hand to reassure her when it appeared Raoul was going to be late. The gesture reminded her that an antique gold wedding band would join her engagement ring within the hour.

Sucking in her breath as the time for the ceremony approached, Emma kept glancing toward the entrance, searching for Raoul's tall dark figure. She prayed her disappointment didn't show as the door opened and Raoul's mother entered the room with his older brother, Etienne, clasping her elbow. He explained that Raoul should be arriving any minute.

"Emma, *ma chère.*" Madeleine Villard made her way with some difficulty to Emma's side. The older woman suffered from arthritis but she always looked regal and elegant, and never more so than she did that afternoon. Her large dark eyes appraised Emma with genuine affection and warmth.

"My son may be too speechless to say his vows when he first sees you." She lifted a fragile hand to Emma's shoulder-length veil. "Thank you for wearing the mantilla. It was handmade by the nuns in Alençon, France. My mother gave it to me on the day of my wedding. I wanted a daughter so I could present it to her. Marie—" she nodded toward Etienne's attractive red-haired wife, who'd just walked in "—wore it at her wedding. Now I have you..." She cleared her throat, then said in a matter-of-fact tone, "The effect of the lace over your blond hair is exquisite."

"You couldn't have given me anything I'd love more." Emma's voice caught. "I'll always treasure it. Perhaps one day I'll be able to give it to our daughter."

"Nothing would make me happier." The woman's eyes misted over. "My son is a lucky man, Emma. I'm sorry his father didn't live long enough to meet you. He would have loved you, too."

"Thank you," Emma whispered, but her anxiety over her husband-to-be's absence made her distracted and restless. "Did you see Raoul this morning? Talk to him?"

"No, but Etienne and the children had breakfast with him, didn't you, *mon fils?*" She turned her head in her son's direction, a man whose features were a softer version of Raoul's. "*Oui, maman,*" he asserted, moving from Marie's side to his mother's. "He'll be here any moment. You mustn't worry so." But Madeleine, like Emma, was concerned and told her youngest son, Roger, to call the house and find out what was keeping Raoul.

"*Bien.*" Roger's brown eyes fastened on Emma with open admiration. "This is one event in my big brother's life he wouldn't miss if he had to be brought in by ambulance, *ma belle.*" He grinned, cocking his handsome, teenage head to the side.

"Roger!" his mother reprimanded him. "This is not the time to tease about such matters." Looking suddenly weary, she sat down in a folding chair Etienne brought her.

"But *maman,* Emma knows I'm only joking." He leapt over to kiss Emma on both cheeks. "I do believe you're really worried about him."

Emma swallowed hard. "I'll feel better when he's here," she admitted in a shaky voice.

"She's been like this since we left Denver yesterday," Lorna chimed in, hugging Emma around her slender waist. "Do her a favor and call, Roger. Otherwise she's going to work herself into a nervous state. Worse than she is now." Lorna smiled, but it didn't reach her light blue eyes. "The ceremony should've begun five minutes ago."

Roger threw his hands in the air. "I'll be right back, but you're worrying for nothing."

"Let's get another picture of you with your family." Etienne positioned himself with a camera as he gestured to Emma.

"Excellent idea," Emma's father murmured as he hugged both daughters to him. Flashes went off. For the next five minutes, pictures were taken in various groupings, but Emma's anxiety had increased so much that she feared something terrible had happened to Raoul. She flew toward Roger when he reentered the room alone.

"No sign of him yet," he informed the group without his characteristic joie de vivre. "He said he had

something important to do concerning the honeymoon before coming to the church. He's probably
been delayed by heavy traffic.''

Madeleine got ponderously to her feet, leaning on
her cane. ''I suggest we phone the hospitals, in case
there's been an accident.''

Emma began to shake and couldn't stop. ''Daddy?
Please call. I have this dreadful feeling something's
wrong.'' He chewed on his lower lip, deep in concentration, then nodded. As he headed toward the door,
the pastor came into the room, obviously as anxious
as everyone else.

''What shall we do?'' Emma beseeched him.

The pastor eyed her with compassion. ''Why not
wait another half hour, to give Raoul time to arrive.
Surely something unavoidable is keeping him. In the
meantime, I'll inform the guests that there's been a
slight delay.''

As he turned to leave, a buzzing noise in Emma's
ears added to the sensation that the world was receding from her.

''Emma!'' Etienne cried out in alarm as the blood
drained from her face. She stood there, bathed in the
red and blue light filtering through the stained glass
windows, but she must have appeared as lifeless as she
felt. Etienne caught her by the shoulders and eased her
into a chair. ''Roger, get Emma some water, *vite!*''

The next few minutes were a blur of activity as everyone attempted to comfort Emma and see to her
needs. Soon, fifteen minutes, then half an hour, had

passed. Still Emma refused to budge from the room. Finally the pastor took on the unpleasant duty of informing the congregation that the groom hadn't arrived.

Long after everyone had gone home, the two families remained at the church, waiting for word, while Etienne and Lorna's husband, Donald, made repeated calls to the police and the various hospitals.

Emma stared blindly into space. Raoul's mother was suffering great distress, but Emma had gone into shock. She felt her father's arm slip around her shoulder to support her.

"Come on, Emma. We'll go back home with Madeleine and Etienne—to wait."

Stiff and cold as marble, Emma allowed herself to be helped out to the car, but even now she didn't remember the twenty-minute ride to the Villard estate. Nor could she recall with any clarity the following couple of weeks, when every conceivable inquiry turned up no answers. Raoul had simply vanished as if he had never been.

When it became definite that Raoul wasn't going to reappear, Emma's father made plans for them to go back to Colorado. But Emma couldn't bear to leave. In a state of near-hysteria, she was sedated by the Villards' family doctor before flying to Denver with her father. The depth of her grief in the ensuing weeks forced him to take her to a doctor for therapy. Gradually her depression had become less acute and she was able to function again.

A moan came from Emma's throat, bringing her back to the present with a start. She moved away from the window, shaken by the memory of Raoul's unexplained disappearance and the ghastly months that followed.

Perhaps it was foolish, but more than ever, she felt she had to see Father John again so she could put the entire incident out of her mind for good.

"Come out, come out, wherever you are." Stephen's voice, booming from the hallway, reached Emma's ears, and she hurried across the room to open the door.

He swept inside with her luggage. "What?" he cried out, hands on his hips. "Still in your parka? There's a fire going in the refectory. It'll warm you."

"I'm glad you're back," she sighed. "Is everything all right? Dame Margaret?"

"She's still asleep, and the Wagoneer is on its way to the next town for repairs. The dents are sizable, but I think they can be pounded out." His eyes played over her face. "You look a little pale. Father André said you weren't feeling well when Father John brought you here."

Emma retrieved a brush from her overnight case and ran it through her curls to disguise her strange mood. "I'm fine, just hungry."

He put his hands on her shoulders. "So am I. How about an appetizer to sustain me on the way to the dining room?"

He seemed to be waiting for her consent before he bent to kiss her. Emma could tell he wanted to take up where he'd left off in the Jeep. But the incident with Father John had disturbed her too deeply; she knew now that she couldn't pretend feelings for Stephen she didn't have. Her preoccupation must have communicated itself to him for he lifted his head, not asking the question that was in his eyes. "Ready?"

She nodded and put her hand through his arm. As far as she could tell, the abbey had no other guests at the moment. Stephen explained that it was too late in the season for clients. When the roads were more passable after the spring thaw, potential buyers from all over the world would come to the abbey to purchase its famous Saint Bernards.

Emma cast furtive glances down corridors leading off in different directions, hoping to catch a glimpse of Father John. He was fast becoming an obsession with her.

For the past year she'd conditioned herself not to fall apart every time she saw a tall man with black hair in a crowd of people. But the priest bore such a striking resemblance to Raoul that she couldn't dismiss the possibility—that he *was* Raoul—out of hand.

"This way, please." Father André led them into the functional dining area. "I hope you'll enjoy the fare."

They sat down at a rectangular wood table near the fire. Stephen helped her off with her parka. A tureen of hot soup with hearty beef chunks and vegetables was brought to the table by Father André himself.

Emma savored its delicious odor, and suddenly she felt hungry. A cheese plate and hot sourdough bread fresh from the oven looked enticing. She and Stephen tucked into their meal, enjoying glasses of California wine, and the hollow feeling inside her vanished.

Stephen's eyebrow lifted. "Just what the doctor ordered, wouldn't you agree?"

Emma swallowed the last of her Gruyère cheese. "I didn't know food could taste so good, but the wine has made me sleepy. Do you mind if we have an early night? I'm exhausted."

Her body felt like a ten-ton weight, and her movements were lethargic. Besides, Emma doubted she'd have an opportunity to see any of the priests that night. Father André appeared to be the only one responsible for guests. She would have to wait until daylight to seek out Father John.

She felt a warm hand clasp hers across the table. "I'm sorry about the accident, Emma." Stephen's lips tightened. "What a way to begin!" He let go of her hand and rose to his feet.

She shook her head. "I don't want to hear another word of apology. This has been an adventure. We can tell everyone back home how we were rescued by the monks in a snowstorm. I wouldn't have missed it for the world." She flashed him a bright smile, then thanked Father André for his hospitality before leaving the refectory.

When they reached her room Stephen rested one hand against the doorjamb. "I hope you don't regret coming here with me." His somber mood worried her.

"Why do you say that?"

He straightened and drew a ragged breath. "Because you're trying so hard. Good night, Emma. Sweet dreams." He ran his fist gently beneath her chin with its hint of a cleft, then went into his own room. A stab of remorse jolted her as she heard his door close.

The events of the past few hours had left her confused and unsettled, but her greatest fear at the moment was hurting Stephen. Their tenuous personal relationship had no hope of blossoming if she couldn't bury the pain of Raoul's disappearance. Even Stephen with all his wonderful qualities wouldn't remain patient much longer.

Emma slid into bed minutes later, plagued by memories she'd tried desperately to suppress. Sleep didn't come for a long time, but she couldn't blame the hard mattress. Her thoughts drifted back to her last outing with Raoul.

It had been one of those glorious fall days in the mountains above Vail, with the sky an intense, vivid blue. Raoul had wanted Emma to himself before he flew to Montreal to get ready for their wedding. They'd taken a basket of food and climbed through wildflowers to a remote meadow nestled between two mountain peaks.

After their picnic, they'd indulged in an interlude of playfulness. She remembered how he'd pelted her with fairy slipper orchids and then kissed her until she'd forgotten where they were. Always before, Raoul had held back in his lovemaking, insisting that he wanted Emma for his wife before he took her to bed for the first time.

But knowing they were to be separated for the entire week before the wedding caused Emma to respond to Raoul's sensual demands with abandon. For the first time in their brief but romantic courtship, Raoul's hunger for her knew no bounds. Trembling, out of control, he whispered that he loved her more than life itself and couldn't wait any longer to make love to her completely. If a group of hikers hadn't chosen that moment to pass by, Emma would have succumbed and known the rapture of his possession.

She could still hear the emotion in his voice and still feel her body throb from the sensations his lovemaking had aroused, even though it had been two years since she'd lain in his arms.

Emma sat up in the bed, her heart pounding unmercifully. Her gaze darted to the white band of skin on her finger where the engagement ring had rested until this trip to the mountains. She'd taken it off for Stephen—to prove that she'd put the past behind her.

Emma closed her eyes on a groan. She'd been so happy, so incredibly happy that day with Raoul. Perhaps she'd had a premonition of disaster, she thought, recalling her panic at the airport. But nothing had prepared her for his sudden disappearance. It was as if he'd evaporated into thin air, leaving no trace of his existence. All efforts by her family and his to discover what had happened to him were futile, and the consensus was that he'd met with some kind of accident or foul play, and died.

For months Emma felt as if she, too, had died. But eventually she forced herself to pick up the pieces of her life and go on to qualify as a vet, only to suffer more anguish almost a year later when her father died suddenly of a heart attack while shoveling snow in front of their house in Denver.

From that point on, Emma had only existed. She'd never ventured near the mountains again and avoided all winter sports. The snow had killed her father prematurely, and it had been the backdrop for her first meeting with Raoul. Two losses so close together had almost destroyed her. She hated winter.

Yesterday's incident with Father John had awakened something inside her—hope or uncertainty? Emma wasn't sure, but she knew she wouldn't be able to rest until she'd seen the priest again. Reliving those moments in the Jeep made her toss and turn for the remainder of the night. Early morning found her wide awake. She sprang out of bed determined to discover Father John's whereabouts before the day was over. Once she'd found him, she'd realize it was a case of mistaken identity. And with the proof before her eyes, she'd be able to exorcise Raoul from her mind and heart.

She and Stephen hadn't made definite plans. Most of the day would be devoted to examining the dogs and giving inoculations. She doubted if Stephen was even up yet. If she hurried, she could explore the abbey and be back in time to have breakfast with him.

She dressed in navy wool pants and a matching sweater, then quietly left the room. Father André was talking to some skiers from the tour bus out front as she entered the vestibule minutes later. He gave her directions to the kennel before accompanying the visitors to the museum.

Emma walked down the corridor he'd pointed out and found the staircase in question. Even if she'd lost her way, the odor from the kennel would have put her back on track. She had a sense of homecoming as she hurried down the steps to the abbey cellars, beautifully redesigned for the dogs.

Scanning the room, she spotted a dozen Saint Bernards at one end. At the other, she saw the pens where the young pups were kept. Their large heads turned in her direction and she smiled. Despite the fact that they'd been bred to survive winter conditions, high altitudes and hard work, the dogs were gentle, loving creatures.

To her surprise Stephen was already working. He darted her a glance from his position at Dame Margaret's side. "You're up early," he commented, sitting back on his haunches to examine the dog's eyes.

Emma entered the pen and took her place at the dog's other side. "I was too excited to sleep." She stroked Dame Margaret's head as her eyes met Stephen's. "She seems none the worse for wear."

He nodded. "I wish I could say the same for you. Your blue eyes don't have that sparkle I like to see. Why don't you go back to bed, Emma."

She bit her lower lip. "Thank you, kind sir, and a top of the morning to you, too."

"Emma..." He reached across Dame Margaret's back and cupped her chin. "You're beautiful even at your worst, but I hate to see you looking so drawn."

"You're the greatest diplomat I know, Stephen." She laughed gently as he removed his hand to check the dog's ears.

"Father Gregory." He motioned to the priest hovering in the background. "Meet Dr. Wakefield, Dr. Holms's replacement from Denver." Emma nodded to the middle-aged priest.

"Dr. Wakefield." He bowed, eyeing her with a certain degree of speculation. She remembered Father André's assessing look the night before, and it occurred to her that maybe Stephen had chosen not to tell the priests about her in case they objected to a woman working on the premises. Instead, he'd insinuated her into the abbey's kennel, presenting her as a fait accompli. If that was so, she had to admire Stephen's clever method of achieving his objective. But as far as she could tell, the priests were accepting her quite readily.

"Would you like to see our prize Saint Bernard?" Father Gregory asked in a friendly voice.

Emma caught Stephen's wink and rose to her feet in anticipation. "I'd be honored. I'm particularly interested in this breed, and I've been looking forward to seeing more of your dogs."

The priest seemed pleased with her remarks. "He's outside right now, enjoying his morning romp in the snow."

Emma's eyes strayed to Dame Margaret. "It appears all your dogs are champions."

"We like to think so."

She trailed him out of the kennel into the overpowering sunlight. She found the glaring brightness almost painful, and it took her a moment to adjust. The huge Saint Bernard came bounding up to the priest.

"Albert, meet a friend." The dog lifted an enormous paw, which Emma shook.

"Oh," she cried, "he's absolutely gorgeous. Aren't you?" She sank to her knees and hugged the dog's neck. He licked her face with his grainy tongue, then started sniffing her hands and sweater.

"Dame Margaret's scent is all over you."

"Yes." Emma burst out laughing. Albert sat still at the priest's command while Emma ran a professional hand and eye over him. "His mask is superb!"

The priest beamed from ear to ear. "He shows a remarkable likeness to the first Barry from the Trappist abbey in the Swiss Alps."

Emma knew all about the ancestor of the renowned alpine mastiffs. "I agree, Father. Their coloring is identical, and he has no spots." Emma rose to her feet, leaning over to inspect the dog's solemn dark eyes. "I've always thought the Saint Bernard was a divine creature. Their pups are like roly-poly cherubs."

He laughed. "Father John says the same thing."

Emma turned away, pretending intense interest in the scenery, but inside she was churning with raw emotion. The priest's remark had triggered something in her memory.

Raoul had adored Emma's Saint Bernard and had witnessed the birth of Gertrude's last litter while he was visiting the Wakefield home. In his subsequent visits, he'd enjoyed watching the pups grow into playful young dogs. There had been three, all of them committed to eager buyers, weeks before their birth. Emma had always been sorry she hadn't kept one for herself—especially when Gertrude died.

Raoul had teased her about her attachment to the puppies. And then in a much more serious tone, he'd promised to provide her with babies just as cherubic to love and cuddle. Her answer had been lost in the fire of his kiss and the hope of fulfillment to come.

"Father?" Emma whirled around. "Father John helped rescue us from the storm last night. I haven't yet had a chance to thank him."

"It's our purpose to help, Dr. Wakefield. When I see him next, I'll tell him. At the moment he's up on the mountain preparing a test area for our newest trainee dogs. It takes several days to get everything ready to put them through maneuvers."

"Would it be possible for me to observe him while he works? I might never have this opportunity again." Her heart began to hammer.

"I'm sorry." He shook his head. "The area is isolated and extremely difficult to reach." He turned, pointing to a distant peak. "In summer you'd be able to stand at the top of the ski lift near the pass, using binoculars to see him work the dogs. Unfortunately winter has set in early this season, and the high winds and sub-zero temperatures make it a virtual impossibility."

"Of course." Emma didn't want to rouse the priest's suspicions over her undue interest in a fellow priest. She patted the handsome dog and shook his paw once more. "Thank you for the introduction, Albert."

Emma chuckled as the dog rubbed his large head against her wool-clad leg. His endearing temperament reminded her forcibly of Gertrude. She sighed regretfully, then excused herself to go back inside the kennel where Stephen was waiting for her.

They spent the rest of the day with the dogs. After dinner, they settled down for a serious game of cards in front of the fire, but Emma's concentration wasn't what it should have been. She was constantly watching for Father John and thinking about him. No, about Raoul... Eventually Stephen declared himself the winner and suggested they visit the museum before calling it a night.

When they reached Emma's door, he kissed her on the forehead, then went to his own room. Emma was thankful he didn't press matters. He'd noticed how preoccupied and on edge she'd been all day, but he'd had the decency to avoid confronting her. Stephen deserved much more than she was capable of giving him.

A little after two in the morning, Emma was still wide awake. Knowing she couldn't go to sleep, she decided to slip back down to the kennel. Working with dogs, being near them, provided a source of comfort and unqualified affection that gave her life purpose and direction. Father André had long since retired for the night, so she moved unnoticed to the lower level of the abbey.

Now that they knew her scent, the dogs showed only mild interest as she entered the kennel. Only one of the oil lamps ranged along the wall had been lit, casting the interior of the room into shadow.

Emma went into Dame Margaret's pen and knelt at her side, stroking her back gently. The dog lifted her head from her paws to lick Emma's hand. Then the back door opened and closed, the sound echoing in the kennel's quiet. Surprised that anyone would still be up at this hour, Emma remained motionless. Through the bars of the pen she caught sight of one of the priests stamping snow from his feet and divesting himself of his hooded parka and gloves. Even in the dim light she could see he was too tall to be Father Gregory.

Adrenaline started to pump through her veins as she followed his movements. He appeared to be making rounds, going from one pen to the next. It was when she heard him speak in soothing French to the dogs that her heart pounded heavily in her ears, and she knew she'd come to the end of her search.

CHAPTER THREE

RAOUL WAS ALIVE!

Shocked into immobility, Emma stayed rooted to the spot, scarcely able to credit the evidence before her eyes. How long had he been a monk? Had he always had a vocation for the priesthood?

Emma felt a searing pain deep in her chest and she suddenly found breathing difficult. On the morning of their wedding day, he must have made the choice to serve God rather than live the rest of his life with her. How long had he been contemplating such a move? Why had he waited until everyone was assembled at the church to turn his back forever on the people who loved him? His actions defied reason, yet here he was, bigger than life.

As he moved closer, the pain ripping her apart slowly turned into the white heat of anger. Physically he was still the same Raoul, except for the unfamiliar beard, but two years had changed him in other ways not so easily discernible. There was a brooding detachment about him, a cold severity she'd never seen before.

Unable to stand the suspense a moment longer, she called out to him. "Father John!"

He straightened to his full height with an abruptness that told Emma he'd been caught off guard. He'd obviously thought himself alone, because his body had tensed at the sound of her voice.

"Madam?" He spoke warily. His back was to the light, and his tall frame was merely a dark shape, a silhouette.

"May I speak to you for a moment?" She got clumsily to her feet.

There was the slightest hesitation before he said, with scarcely concealed impatience, "The public is not allowed in the kennel after hours. If you wish to see the dogs, make arrangements with Father André in the morning."

She started to shiver. "Raoul?" she whispered. "I-it's Emma!"

She heard his sharp intake of breath, saw the way he seemed, for an infinitesimal moment, to stagger at the revelation. "So it *was* you . . ."

She thought she sensed pain in that deeply voiced utterance reverberating in the warm silence of the kennel.

She moved out of Dame Margaret's pen, but Raoul's formidable stance caused her to approach him fearfully. Closer now, she could make out his dark brows and his eyes, more black than brown. The full beard and mustache hid his strong jawline and arrogant mouth, a mouth that could soften with tenderness.

His skin had darkened, from exposure to sun and wind, no doubt. She thought he seemed leaner beneath the snow pants and bulky sweater he wore. In knee-high boots, he made an imposing figure, with a primitive male strength and beauty that took her breath away.

"Last night I thought I was seeing things, too," she murmured, staring straight at him. She couldn't identify the forbidding stranger in front of her with the man who'd relentlessly pursued her from the moment he'd seen her walking through the lobby of the ski lodge at Vail.

After a tension-filled moment, he asked in a strangely flat voice, "Are you engaged to Dr. Channing?"

Emma's chest heaved with the weight of her anguish. That he could even mention another man at a time like this destroyed what little self-control she had left. "No—but it would ease your conscience if I said yes, wouldn't it?"

She could no longer disguise the bitterness pent up inside. "Of course, I don't need to ask you the same question. Your presence at the abbey speaks for itself." Her chin lifted a fraction. "A mere woman couldn't hope to compete with God, could she?"

Raoul stood with his hands clenched at his sides. He gazed at her, eyes veiled, obviously studying her short golden curls, the high cheekbones and full mouth. Emma knew he was making mental comparisons with the way she'd looked when he'd last seen her. The change was dramatic. At twenty-three, she'd worn her hair long and flowing. Once he'd gazed on the full curves of her slender body in male admiration. Now, two years later, he could undoubtedly tell that she needed to put on weight.

"What are you doing here, Emma? How did you know where to find me?" came the terse demand. He'd abruptly made himself the interrogator, as if *she* was the guilty party.

"That's *all* you have to say to me after the nightmare I've been living for the past two years? Knowing nothing? Imagining anything and everything?" she cried angrily. "To think that all this time you've only been a couple of hours from Denver! I can't take it in."

She paused. "It's so strange," she went on in a tremulous voice. "When everyone said you had to be dead, I never quite believed it. I considered every possible reason under the sun for your disappearance. But I have to admit that finding you *here* would never have occurred to me in a million years."

At her words, he closed his eyes for a moment, as if he were putting up with a recalcitrant child. This only added fuel to her anger. "My trespassing in your world wasn't part of the plan was it, Raoul? You thought you were safe in your isolated aerie, content to shrink from the responsibilities of life. Well, I have news for you. You're a mortal like the rest of us. And you owe me and your family an explanation, even if you are a priest!"

A shadow crossed his face and he reached out and grasped her wrist, holding her fast. "Who told you I was here? Answer me!" He shook her, not gently.

Emma's dark-fringed blue eyes grew huge. She didn't begin to know the man who inhabited Raoul's body. "No one told me. I'm the new vet who replaced Dr. Holms at Dr. Channing's clinic in Denver. We came to do routine exams of the dogs and return Dame Margaret. How could I possibly have known you were here?" Her voice broke. "I—we all thought you were dead!" To her horror, tears filled her eyes as her mournful cry echoed against the stone walls. The dogs whimpered uneasily before settling down again.

"Mon Dieu," Raoul groaned, his grip tightening until Emma winced from the pressure. "Are you telling me the truth?"

She nodded helplessly. "Why would I lie? I must be the only person in the world, aside from the priests, who even knows you're alive—let alone has any idea where you are at this moment. I thought it was you when I climbed out of the Jeep last night, but until I heard you speaking French a few minutes ago, I couldn't be positive."

His black eyes swept over her. "Did you mention your suspicions to anyone else?" He still held her shackled to him as he continued his questioning.

"I didn't dare say anything because I thought I was losing my mind. Maybe I'm in the middle of one of my nightmares right now and can't wake up."

He seemed suddenly to realize that he was exerting too much strength, and he let go of her. She rubbed her wrist absently. "It might as well be a nightmare," he told her roughly. "When you leave this place with Dr. Channing, I want your promise before God that you'll never reveal what you found here to a living soul."

Emma stared at him as if she'd never seen him before. "You can't mean that. Do you have any idea what your unexplained disappearance did to us?" Her voice caught from emotion. "The Raoul Villard I once knew couldn't possibly be so cruel. Your poor mother and brothers deserve to know you're alive. You can't imagine what it's been like for them. For all of us.

"At first we thought you'd been in an accident, but there was no evidence of that at all. Then we wondered if you were suffering from a terminal illness and wanted to spare everyone the pain— but you're obviously in good health. Correct me if I'm wrong, but it stands to reason that only priests of extraordinary physical well-being and stamina can survive here."

Emma waited, but he said nothing, did nothing. He might have been made of the same hard granite that formed the walls of the abbey. "Raoul," she half sobbed, frantic at his continued reticence, "why couldn't you have told me you wanted to be a priest? Did I seem such a shallow person you thought I wouldn't understand? You can tell me the truth. Why not do it now and be done with it? They say confession is good for the soul, or does being a priest make you exempt?''

His refusal to explain anything about his motives was driving her to the edge. "Did you have so little faith in me that you thought I'd try to prevent you from taking vows? Is that it? If only you'd told me, if you'd even hinted, we could have talked it out. Why didn't you?'' In exasperation she grasped his arms, wild with rage because he wouldn't explain himself. "Answer me, damn you! Help me understand!''

His dark eyes glittered dangerously as he stared at her, then he dropped his gaze in pointed fashion to her hand, which held him fast. His mouth thinned and he pulled sharply away from her grip. Too late she remembered he was Father John, that he'd taken vows of chastity. A woman's love was one of the many things he'd willingly given up for the cloistered life.

She backed away. This close, his touch, his male warmth still had the power to disturb her. She couldn't help but wonder if her nearness affected him the same way, but he seemed to have iron control over his emotions and displayed no feelings at all.

"Raoul Villard is dead,'' he said in a voice totally devoid of expression. "Let him stay dead, or you'll cause untold pain to all those you purport to love. Do you want that on your conscience, or has Emma Wakefield become too selfish to think about anyone but herself? Two years don't seem to have changed your impetuosity.''

His brutal remark was as hurtful as if he'd physically slapped her across the room. She'd never thought of herself as impulsive. Had Raoul found that trait so unattractive he couldn't imagine spending the rest of his life with her?

Stephen had accused her of being exactly the opposite. But then Stephen hadn't known her when she was deeply in love with a man whose skiing career made impossible demands on his time. It seemed her relationship with Raoul had been based on a string of stolen moments. They'd rarely had more than a few days together at a time, and she'd clung to those precious hours, lived for them. Had he found her emotional dependence on him too cloying?

She'd wanted the truth, but somehow she hadn't expected it to come in this form and be delivered with such debilitating force. "So," she said in a dull voice, "it was something lacking in me, after all, and at the last minute you couldn't face me. Is that it?"

"Don't, Emma." His voice was a hoarse whisper, and for an unbelievable moment, she thought she saw anguish flicker in the black depths of his eyes before he abruptly turned away. His swift strides took him to the far end of the room, where he disappeared into the shadows, leaving her completely bereft.

No matter that his feelings for her had undergone a drastic change—she could tell he'd suffered. She was suddenly convinced that his pain had been as great as hers. Perhaps greater. It was there in his manner, his voice, his expression. What had happened to him?

Why would a man who'd always been so vital and alive say *Raoul Villard is dead?*

Emma dashed up the stairs after him, stopping on the first landing to listen for his footsteps, but to no avail. The abbey was a masterpiece of passageways and hidden rooms. Raoul could be anywhere by now.

He'd stay away, keep out of sight, until she and Stephen left the mountains. In fact she wouldn't put it past him to relocate to another monastery, leaving no trail to follow. His determination to remain lost to the world would become stronger than ever, but the pain in his eyes would always haunt her if she didn't have answers.

Though he'd done everything in his power to discourage her from trying to make contact with him again, she couldn't let it alone, even if he was a priest. Thanks to Father Gregory, Emma knew where Raoul was hiding in the mountains, and in the morning she'd find him. She'd force him to unburden himself so she could finally get on with living. Discovering that Raoul was alive, in this condition, was worse than anything she'd gone through since his disappearance.

Emma stole back to her room and spent the rest of the night making plans. Sleep was out of the question. Shaking from reaction, she tried to imagine how his family would respond if she ignored Raoul's entreaty and went to them with the unbelievable news that he hadn't died, after all.

How could she tell his mother he'd been living in a monastery close to Denver all this time, yet as far away from civilization as it was possible to get? And worse, that he didn't want to be found because he'd renounced his old life. Emma couldn't fathom it, couldn't accept it.

According to Father André, a free tour bus from the Snowdrift ski resort, about two miles away, stopped at the abbey twice daily. The skiers enjoyed a cup of hot chocolate, browsed in the museum and visited the kennel, leaving a small donation that helped finance the abbey. Emma intended to join them, and she lay down on the bed to think through her bold plan. Morning came slowly.

At seven o'clock, she descended the stairs to the vestibule. "Father André?" she said. "Would you please tell Dr. Channing I'm going to ride to the ski area with the tour group visiting the abbey? I want to get in a few runs as long as I'm here. Another tour bus will bring me back at noon, which is the time Dr. Channing and I agreed to get to work."

"I wouldn't recommend it, Dr. Wakefield," he said kindly, but she felt the steel behind his words.

In some nebulous way he'd changed since the day before. His warning compelled her to ask, "Why is that, Father?"

"A wind has already come up and there'll be a bad storm later. The lift might even be closed already. You'd be wise to remain inside."

If that was the case, why were skiers boarding the bus in front of the hotel at this very moment? Had

Raoul told Father André to detain her? "I'll risk it in hopes that conditions aren't as bad as you fear."

Though he did nothing overt, she could tell her response displeased him. "I wouldn't advise it. Frostbite is not an uncommon occurrence. Your face and extremities must be protected at all times."

"I'll be careful. Thank you." Emma started to turn away, then remembered. "Father? I notice you have binoculars for rent. I'd like to take a pair along if you don't mind?"

He paused, but then he said, "Certainly," and accommodated her with field glasses in a well-worn case. She put five dollars in the donation basket and hurried outside to retrieve her skis and poles from the Wagoneer, doing her best to ignore his inquisitive stare. Was guilt for what she was about to do written all over her face? Had Raoul alerted the other priests to keep a close eye on her, to prevent her from coming anywhere near him?

Determinedly, she headed for the bus, placing her skis and poles with those of the others who were going up the lift in search of fresh powder from the previous storm. With luck, Stephen would stay asleep for several more hours and not miss her.

Emma counted a handful of tourists among the skiers, all of whom appeared enthusiastic and friendly. Emma was invited to sit down next to a rather attractive, huskily built blond man from Colorado Springs named Kyle Rawlings who immediately informed her that he loved to ski. He wasted no time trying to get to know her.

By the time they'd arrived at the bottom of the lift, he'd told her he was staying at the Snowdrift and asked her to join him for fondue that evening. Emma refused, explaining that she and Stephen were at the abbey on a working holiday. But even if she'd been free, his type didn't interest her. He was too aggressive, too sure of himself; he irritated Emma by walking with her to the lift lineup.

In front of everyone he held out his hand, beckoning her to ride the double chair with him. To her frustration, Emma had no choice but to sit next to him. Thankfully the rapidly deteriorating weather made conversation virtually impossible.

Father André had spoken the truth about the wind. It cut through her three layers of protection, but Emma was only vaguely aware of the biting cold. The gray sky with its menacing black clouds moving in from the north matched her mood as the lift carried them high above jutting rocks and precipices to the frozen glacier at the top.

Unzipping the front of her parka, she raised the rented binoculars to her eyes. The sight of peak after peak knifing skyward in the frozen wilderness made her gasp. She was moving through space up to the top of the world, a fascinating and completely alien panorama of ice and snow.

Her eyes strained for any sign of movement as she scanned the treacherous terrain. Raoul was out here somewhere. She had to find him! The people operating the lift had said this would be the last run for the day because of the approaching storm. When the blizzard was over, Raoul could be gone forever.

Remembering what Father Gregory had said, she trained the glasses immediately below the peak to her far right. Her hands shook with nervous excitement as she caught sight of something moving across a narrow ledge in the far distance. She held her breath until another dark speck appeared, then another. The dogs!

Emma put the field glasses away, zipping her parka and slipping her goggles into place. Kyle raised his ski poles in the air, indicating their turn to exit the lift was next. She nodded and prepared to do so, hoping to disappear before anyone had a chance to miss her.

Luck was with her. When Kyle bent over his skis to adjust the bindings, she took the opportunity to elude him, confident that everyone would be too busy to notice her departure from the group. The area cordoned off for skiers lay to the left; Emma skied her way around a huge outcropping of rocks on the right.

The binoculars had made Raoul and the dogs seem almost close. Without binoculars, she couldn't even see them, and when she looked across the endless frozen ridge she had to traverse, her heart dropped to her feet. Danger signs, in six different languages, had been posted here, but she swept past them, driven by an urgency she'd never felt before.

If she didn't confront Raoul today, she might never see him again—might never be able to find him again. She couldn't take that chance. She needed to know why he'd run away instead of telling her the truth, whatever it was. She'd never have a moment's peace if she didn't get an answer.

Another sign warned that to proceed farther meant doing so at one's own peril. Emma glanced at the sign, dug her poles into the snow for leverage and shoved off across a sea of ice, a ripplelike flow of glacier across broken ground.

Her skis flew along the wind-sculpted ridge as it rounded the mountainside, but then it disappeared before it rose suddenly on the other side and she was forced to sidestep to reach the edge. She couldn't seem to get enough oxygen into her starved lungs. Strong gusts of wind blew the top layer of snow into the thin air, blinding her vision, chilling her to the bone.

She pulled off her glove with her teeth and drew out the binoculars once more, but it was wasted energy because she couldn't see anything. The ridge blended into the white all around her. She couldn't tell where ice and snow met the sky.

A low ceiling of clouds obscured the top of the lift, making her feel totally alone. Only the knowledge that Raoul and the dogs were working on the other side of the ice field gave her the impetus to keep going.

She knew the ridge was full of hidden abysses, crevices and fissures. Before each glide of her skis, she sank her ski pole into the snow-encrusted ice immediately ahead of her. The process was painstaking and robbed her of strength. Sometimes a whole section of ice gave way and slid down the steep slope, terrifying her.

She lost all sense of time. She was perhaps halfway across the ridge when snow started to fall. It didn't settle gently, descending, rather, as if it was being poured from the heavens. A full-fledged blizzard enveloped Emma, disorienting her, suffocating her. She was paralyzed by fear until she recalled Raoul's advice. *Concentrate! One step at a time. Don't think about anything else!* She could almost hear his voice....

Summoning courage from some inner reserve, Emma felt her way through the snow-covered ice, inch by inch, testing it to see if it would support her weight. She told herself Raoul couldn't be far from her now.

At one point, exhaustion overtook her, and she stopped for breath, leaning heavily on her poles. She had no idea how long she rested in that position, but as she set off again, the wind changed. It died down a little, and for the first time since starting across the ice field, she could see Raoul on a distant crag, surrounded by four dogs. He must have noticed her struggles because he started waving his hands over his head, as if to warn her away.

In this storm, she couldn't possibly go back. It was vital she reach the section of jutting rocks that would shield her from the force of the elements. She pressed doggedly forward, disregarding Raoul's warning gestures. He represented safety and security.

She focused on him and felt her heart swell with gratitude that she wasn't alone. He wouldn't let anything happen to her. Emma's mind was empty of every other thought. She had to get to Raoul. Raoul would keep her safe.

Giant plumes of powder spouted upward as he came slowly toward her, still motioning frantically with his hands for her to stop. She thought she could hear the dogs barking, but it might have been the screaming of the wind through the chutes and gullies of the summit.

Only one more white, dunelike mound and she'd reach hard rock. Calling on every ounce of strength she could muster, Emma edged her way to the top, but when she got there, she collapsed, and her exhausted body sank to the ice. She was so tired she wanted just to lie there, to fall into a long, warm sleep. Her body began to slide downward, but she didn't have the energy to catch herself.

The storm literally attacked her and she lost any sense of direction. When one of the dogs caught hold of her parka collar to prevent further movement, she could hardly believe it and lifted her head. A figure approached. "Raoul, thank God," she cried, extending a gloved hand to touch the edge of his snowshoe.

CHAPTER FOUR

HARD, ANGRY HANDS gripped her by the armpits and pulled her to a standing position, shaking her. He towered over her, momentarily shielding her from the blowing, icy snow. *"Mon Dieu,"* he muttered. "I knew it was you coming across that glacier. I knew it."

He sounded furious, Emma thought numbly. But any emotion was better than the obdurate facade he'd presented earlier.

"I've got to get you out of this storm. Put your arm around my neck and hang on," he commanded, grasping both her ski poles in one hand. "And don't you dare go to sleep on me!"

"I promise I won't," Emma whispered, trembling with weakness and relief as she felt an arm of whipcord strength hug her around the waist and sweep her along the ridge. She couldn't see an inch in front of her. How could Raoul possibly tell where they were going? Then she realized that the dogs were forging the trail immediately ahead of them.

Emma did her best to keep up and not be a burden, but her legs still felt like rubber, and she was chilled to the bone. But with Raoul holding her fast, she was hardly aware of her danger.

Raoul didn't speak, and she knew he was conserving all his strength to concentrate on the task. She wondered where he could be leading her to find shelter.

"We climb from here," he explained as they reached a precipice. After extricating himself from his snowshoes, he leaned over and unfastened her bindings, helping her step out of her skis.

He left their things in the snow and picked her up in a fireman's lift, carrying her effortlessly up the rocky face without any sign of being winded. Before Emma could say a word, he shouldered his way through a narrow wooden door opening into a stone hut. At Raoul's command, the dogs remained outside.

There was a fire in the hearth, and he set her on her feet in front of it. He unzipped her parka, pulling it away from her head, shoulders and down her arms. Next came the field glasses hanging around her neck, then her goggles, hat and gloves.

Without giving her a choice, he guided her to a cot next to the fireplace and forced her back against the mattress. "Lie down," he ordered while he pulled off her ski sweater, then undid her ski bibs, revealing gray ski underwear beneath.

The only light came from the fireplace, making it difficult for her to distinguish the features of the one-room hut. But for the moment her surroundings didn't matter; she was content just to be out of the storm.

Her body felt like a dead weight. At first there was little sensation as Raoul drew off her boots and ice-encrusted bibs. After that, he removed her heavy socks to examine her feet. He massaged one, then the other, but the movement came to a sudden stop when he fingered her ankle bracelet.

It had been Raoul's first gift to her, a fragile gold chain with an exquisite enameled heart. The inscription on the back read *Je t'adore.* I love you.

Instantly Emma remembered when he'd given it to her. Judging by his abrupt intake of breath and his stilled fingers, he was remembering, too....

She and her family had just come into the lodge from a day's skiing at Vail when she felt a pair of black eyes sweeping over her in admiration.

Raoul had been staying at the same lodge and asked her to dance later that night at an après-ski party. They'd spent the next day together, and every day after that. Emma had fallen in love with him, and when the two weeks were up and she had to go back to Denver, he'd fastened the chain around her ankle and whispered, "Don't read the inscription until you get home, then promise me you'll put it back on and leave it there forever."

Of course Emma read the message the second Raoul was out of sight. The words had leapt out at her, but her joy changed to uncertainty, then pain, when she heard nothing more from him.

Two months went by. Then one day as she was discussing a medical procedure with another student on their way out of class, she discovered Raoul in the hall, waiting for her. After the long lapse of time since she'd seen him, his actual physical presence left her speechless. They continued to gaze at each other, oblivious to the other students.

He didn't say anything at first. In front of any interested passersby, he knelt before Emma and traced the line of her ankle bracelet with his index finger. She was staring down at him when he lifted his head. Desire for her blazed in his dark eyes, and all he said was, ''Where can we go to be alone, Emma? I have something important to ask you.''

Emma could still hear the deep cadence of his voice, the indescribable emotion. She remembered the urgency of his tone and the touch of his hand. She felt it now, as she'd felt it then.

He finally resumed massaging her feet, with increasing vigor. Gradually she could feel the warmth creep back into them, along with sharp prickles as the circulation improved.

''Oh, that hurts.''

''It's supposed to.'' He drew a woolen blanket from the foot of the cot and wrapped it securely around her. Almost before she could comprehend what was happening, he pressed a canteen to her lips. ''Drink this. It will revive you.'' Emma complied, and took several swallows. The brandy burned its way to her stomach. He waited to make sure she drank every drop, then he turned to put another log on the fire.

Within a few minutes a roaring blaze illuminated the room, giving Emma her first real look at the hut's interior. Wood was stacked to the ceiling at each side of the stone hearth. Heat began to permeate her body and a pleasant languor stole over her.

Raoul straddled a workbench, priming a camp stove. The movement gave her a few moments to study his lean, masculine form. She noted he didn't wear a cross, unless it was hidden beneath his clothes. Even in snow pants and serviceable maroon sweater, he possessed a careless grace, an elegance, that easily made him the most attractive man she'd ever known. But the inner man was an inscrutable stranger and she didn't have the faintest idea how to reach him.

The wind howled relentlessly and seemed to be growing in intensity. She shivered as she remembered collapsing on the ridge. If Raoul hadn't seen her coming, she'd surely have frozen to death there, and her body would probably have never been found.

Emma sat up on the cot to watch him. He opened several packets of soup and heated liquid—melted snow, perhaps—in a small pan. He hadn't spoken except to give orders. She wondered how long they might be at the hut together. At least, he couldn't ignore her indefinitely! The storm had isolated them from the world for a little while. Their enforced intimacy would be the last thing Raoul wanted, but the situation suited Emma. He'd never abandon her under the circumstances, and sooner or later he'd be forced to talk to her.

"That smells wonderful," Emma remarked, suspecting that any conversation on her part angered him. He only glanced at her over his broad shoulder. "I didn't have time for anything more than a cup of hot chocolate this morning.''

She knew at once she shouldn't have mentioned not eating breakfast. He would find her foolishness at not downing a hearty meal before she went up the mountain inexcusable. His veiled black eyes, mere slits in the firelight, said as much as he stared at her for an uncomfortably long moment before he poured the steaming liquid into mugs. He approached the cot and handed her one, nodding brusquely at her murmured thanks.

While she sipped the tomato soup, he tidied the hut and hung her things over a chair to dry near the hearth. "I'll be back soon," he muttered, putting on his heavy parka. In a few economical movements, he reached the door and went out into the blizzard.

Just opening and closing the door for a second brought a blast of frigid air inside, reminding her of the blinding tempest all around them. The stone hut was a miraculous hideaway, a small, low-ceilinged room that provided refuge from the elements.

Emma felt perfectly safe and comfortable. In fact, the room was becoming too warm. She pushed back the blankets and took off her sweater. Her gray ski underwear would have to serve as her clothing for the time being. It covered her from wrist to ankle.

She got up from the cot and walked barefoot across the cold planking to another chair, where she placed her sweater. With real interest, she looked around the hut. The opposite wall was lined with stores and provisions of all kinds: mountaineering equipment, packs, sleeping bags, lanterns, all neatly arranged.

A battered duffel bag in the corner drew her gaze. Maybe Raoul had a pair of heavy socks she could wear until hers were dry. She didn't think he'd mind and she bent over to look inside. To her surprise she found a dozen or more paperback novels, along with a deck of playing cards packed in with a couple of well-worn tracksuits and sweatshirts.

Emma blinked. Was a priest allowed to read fiction? Or play cards, for that matter? She had no conception of a priest's life. She wasn't surprised that he didn't wear a habit like Father André. It would be ridiculous to imagine the monks donning priestly garb to work in the mountains with the dogs. Maybe the books and cards had been left behind by a stranded victim of a storm such as this.

"What do you think you're doing?"

Emma whirled around as if she'd been struck and eyed him guiltily. Raoul had come back to the hut carrying the snowshoes and skis they'd left at the base of the rocks. She stood up, conscious of his dark eyes scrutinizing her disheveled mop of curls. There'd been a time when he'd likened her long, silky mane of hair to spun gold, and begged her never to cut it.

The ski underwear covered her but didn't really conceal her body. He couldn't help but notice the weight loss. For two years, Emma hadn't given a thought to her looks or her figure, and it showed.

"I thought I might borrow a pair of socks until mine are dry," she explained, almost as an afterthought.

He moved to the corner and rested the equipment against the stone wall. "I hoped you'd have enough sense to stay under the blanket. You could have died of exposure out there," he said in a deceptively quiet voice as he took off his gloves and parka.

"You reached me too quickly for that to happen. I feel fine," Emma asserted. But she hurried back to the cot, pulling the covers up to her chin.

He flashed her an unreadable glance before producing a thick pair of gray socks from a water-resistant bag hanging on a peg. With that swift grace peculiar to him, he moved to the cot and untucked a corner of the blanket. He crouched down, lifting her feet to examine them in the full light of the fire.

Emma's eyes closed at the heavenly feel of his hands. Their touch sent a wave of warmth through her body. But he was a priest, she reminded herself quickly; she had no right to react this way. Still, it was all she could do not to moan her disappointment when he put socks where his hands had been. Then he replaced the blanket.

Their eyes met; she could hardly breathe because of the strange expression on his face. "Whatever possessed you to start across that glacier? Didn't you read the signs?" he bit out. "You could've plunged to your death a hundred times on your way across."

Emma shivered and looked away, still too shaken by the reality of his presence to ponder her actions.

"I've never known anyone to traverse that ridge. Not even the other priests," he added gravely.

"I didn't think about the danger. The only thing I had on my mind was reaching you."

A long silence stretched between them, and it seemed to her that his skin lost color. "It's a miracle you didn't panic," he said quietly. She must have imagined the tinge of admiration in his voice.

"Not a miracle. I learned from you." She feasted her eyes on his handsome face. "I remembered what you taught me when we were caught in a storm that time at Beaver Creek." She swallowed hard. "That, plus the fact that I knew you were on the other side of the glacier got me through."

He grimaced and rubbed the back of his bronzed neck. She could see new worry lines at the side of his straight nose and radiating from the corners of his eyes. Lines that hadn't been there two years ago. He had a gaunt look that convinced her he'd undergone something traumatic.

His full beard and mustache camouflaged the lower half of his face. Emma had the urge to shave it off so she could see the masculine contours that were once so familiar to her. It took all her strength not to reach out and touch him.

His eyes narrowed on her face. "Do you have any idea how many crevasses are hidden throughout that glacier, just waiting to swallow you alive?" he asked harshly. "One false move would have meant instant death. My heart almost failed me when I saw you struggling."

Emma sat up in the cot, still clutching the covers to her chest. "Nothing happened."

"That's not the point."

She swallowed hard. "No, of course it isn't. What I did was wrong because I put your life in danger. As for my own life, death would have been preferable to living another day without answers now that I know you're alive." She added, "If you hadn't run away from me last night, none of this would've happened."

An angry laugh broke from his throat. "How like a woman to twist the situation!"

His taunt infuriated her. "I'm not just any woman, Raoul, and I still have your diamond ring to prove it. I know you loved me *once,* but something happened to change that. I want to know what it was. I *have* to know!" she pleaded. "That's why I came after you. Don't you understand?"

His mouth had a pinched, white look about it. Unexpectedly he rose to his full, imposing height and stared down at her with a forbidding expression. "I understand that your actions of this morning have sent out an alarm at the abbey."

Emma lowered her eyes, only now beginning to realize the consequences of her impulsive behavior. Naturally the news of her disappearance would have reached the monastery. Stephen would be frantic and the priests would be forced to put aside their chores to look for her. She hadn't thought beyond finding Raoul. It had simply never occurred to her that her actions might cause distress and inconvenience, or worse. She was shocked at her own recklessness and self-absorption.

Full of remorse, she smoothed a trembling hand through her blond curls. "I didn't mean to worry anyone! I had no idea the storm would prevent me from getting back to the abbey. All I wanted was an opportunity to talk to you, away from the others. I was afraid you'd leave the monastery for another one and I'd never be able to trace you. I couldn't let that happen without trying to appeal to you one more time." She shook her head. "I'm sorry to be responsible for so much upheaval."

His frown intensified. "What makes the situation worse is the fact that I lost my pocket radio somewhere on the glacier, so I can't contact the sanctuary to let them know you're all right. As soon as you're settled, I'll take the dogs out with me and we'll try to find it. Pray that we do. Otherwise, when the storm lifts every available priest will be called on a search for you, not to mention your Dr. Channing, who must be out of his mind with worry."

"He's not *my* Dr. Channing." Her lips quivered. "But he is my boss and a wonderful person. I would never hurt him intentionally."

Turning away, he stoked the fire with his boot and added more logs, obviously concerned about maintaining a comfortable temperature for her.

She still couldn't believe she'd found him, that he was alive and actually standing a few feet away. Close enough to touch... "Raoul," she began in a tremulous voice. "Please—on the strength of the love we once shared—tell me why you couldn't marry me. I won't fall apart with the answer. I swear it! You have my word I'll leave here as soon as I can and never look back. Just tell me what I need to know." Her throat closed then, and she could feel the tears gathering.

When he didn't say anything, Emma threw off the covers and jumped to the floor. She crossed to stand next to him before the blazing fire, but he didn't appear to notice.

Emma rubbed the back of her hand across her eyes and swallowed with difficulty. She began again. "I accept the fact that you've made a new life for yourself, here in the mountains you love. But when you made that choice, you turned my life into a big question mark. I even consulted a psychiatrist to try to deal with the pain."

Raoul shifted his weight. "Why do you continue to torture yourself?"

"Wouldn't you, if our positions were reversed? If I'd been the one to disappear, don't you think your life would've been altered?" she cried, willing him to look at her. "Maybe a woman is different. Maybe I'm different. Obviously I loved you too much!" She swallowed a sob. "You were my whole life!"

"That's not true. You went on to qualify as a vet."

"Only after months of counseling." It was impossible to disguise the horror of that period. "The doctor told me I had to find something else in life to care about. Eventually I took my boards and Stephen hired me. This was meant to be a working holiday. It took me a month to summon the courage to come to the mountains. Stephen challenged me to face my pain and put your memory to rest once and for all. I thought I'd succeeded. . . ." Her voice trailed off.

He started to say something, then suddenly yanked his parka from the wall and shrugged into it.

"You're going out *now?*" Emma had visions of him disappearing in the storm, never to return.

"It's imperative the dogs and I find that radio. While we're gone you need to rest. You almost froze to death today. Go back to bed and stay there," he ordered with such authority that she didn't dare argue. In fact, she was feeling distinctly light-headed and she willingly enough climbed back into the cot. Still, it galled her that Raoul obviously had no intention of answering her questions.

"I won't be gone long," he said with restored calm, reading her fears correctly. Then he headed out into the blizzard again. She could hear the dogs as they greeted him. The second he closed the door, Emma threw her pillow against it. His refusal to talk to her made her angry, perhaps angrier than she'd ever been in her life. She knew she was on the verge of hysteria but couldn't seem to stop herself from reacting.

However, exhaustion, plus the high altitude, finally caught up with her and she slept.

Some time later, she awoke to the sensation that she was no longer alone. When she heard Raoul call her softly, she knew he'd been standing by the cot watching her, but she didn't respond. She derived a perverse pleasure from ignoring *him* for a change and nestled deeper into the pillow.

Belatedly she realized that when he'd returned, he must have found her pillow by the door and put it beneath her head while she slept. The thought that he'd seen evidence of her tantrum caused a wave of heat to wash over her. Never again would she allow herself to lose control like that.

He repeated her name, more urgently this time, and she felt compelled to turn over and sit up. She was immediately aware that he'd lighted the lantern, and she rubbed her eyes with her knuckles at the unexpected brightness. If she didn't know better, she'd have thought he sounded anxious. "What is it? Couldn't you find your radio?"

He studied her features through narrowed eyes. "Unfortunately, no. The dogs tracked it to a deep crevasse too narrow for me to enter. But right now I'm more concerned about you. You've been asleep too long for someone who's had nothing substantial to eat in the last twelve hours. At this altitude it's important to keep up your strength."

He sounded very much like a doctor. "I guess I needed the rest, as you said." She glanced at her watch to see the time and noticed to her dismay that it was missing. She'd probably lost it crossing the glacier. Judging by Raoul's scowl, he'd surmised the same thing.

"It's after nine and time for dinner. I have a hot meal ready. Don't get up," he cautioned when she started to remove the blanket. "I'll bring it to you."

"I don't want you waiting on me."

He darted her a furious glance. "The warmest place in the hut is right where you are. After what you've been through today, your resistance is dangerously low, so you'll take care of yourself. *Tu comprends?*" He switched to informal French all of sudden, letting Emma know, as clearly as if he'd said so, that he demanded her unquestioning obedience.

"I understand," Emma muttered then bit her lip and stared moodily into the flames. Deftly he brought her a bowl of thick stew and more of the bread, which he explained was baked daily at the abbey.

"Thank you," she muttered, not looking up at him. "I realize you weren't expecting company, so I hope I'm not depriving you."

"Being prepared for the unexpected is the abbey's top priority," he responded calmly. "A helicopter brings supplies here periodically, so I'm well stocked."

After finishing his meal, he settled down to repair one of the snowshoes she'd seen hanging on the wall. Neither of them spoke for some time. Emma continued to eat, slowly and methodically. Under other circumstances, she would have found the lamb stew delicious, but right now she was too aware of Raoul and the tensions that were building toward some kind of explosion.

"More?" he asked when he saw she'd finished eating, but Emma shook her head. He put his work away, then took the bowl from her and returned with a mug. "This is apple juice. Drink as much as you can so you won't dehydrate."

She drank thirstily; the juice tasted deliciously sweet and tangy. "Thank you." He removed the mug and started to put things away in the corner of the hut serving as a makeshift kitchen. It frustrated her that he continued to wait on her. But she knew it would only anger him further if she tried to be useful.

At some point she was going to make him talk to her. She decided it would have to be when he'd run out of things to do so he'd be forced to go to bed. That reminded her she was using his cot.

"If you'll let me borrow that bedroll I can see propped in the corner," she said, "I'll sleep in front of the hearth for the rest of the night."

His black eyes flashed angrily. "You'll stay exactly where you are. The floor is the surest way for you to end up with pneumonia."

"That goes for priests, as well," she retorted.

She noticed a betraying motion of his hand on the snowshoe before he thundered, "I'm acclimatized. You're not! Now it's time for bed."

Once again his dictates infuriated her, but she'd promised herself to stay in control. "After sleeping all day, I'm not the least bit tired." She studied his brusque movements as he spread his sleeping bag in front of the hearth. She saw that her comment had angered him, and she smiled grimly to herself when he reached for his parka.

"Running away again?" she baited him as he headed for the door.

"Because of you I haven't had a chance to see to the dogs yet." He went outside, slamming the door behind him. Suitably chastened, Emma sank back on the cot. She despaired of their impossible situation and doubted she'd be able to find a chink in that impenetrable armor of his.

Some time later, the door opened and she felt the freezing air swirl in with the dogs. Their pants and whimpers were oddly reassuring. She heard Raoul command them to lie down in front of the fire next to him.

One of the young males was inordinately curious, however, and padded over to Emma. He licked the hand closest to him. Though his short, thick fur coat was damp with snow, Emma instinctively hugged him around the neck.

"Fabrice!" Raoul called out in an authoritative voice. *"Viens ici. Viens!"*

"Let him stay by me," Emma implored. "What can it hurt?"

"For one thing he'll drip water all over you. For another, he's the one who saved you from sliding any farther today. It appears he considers you his private property, but it's best he doesn't become attached."

"Let him stay by me," she pleaded again, strangely touched by Raoul's remark. "He reminds me a little of Gertrude the way he plops his head on the mattress." She smiled wistfully in remembrance and rubbed the dog's head.

"Do you still have her?" he asked after a sustained silence.

"No." She cleared the tightness in her throat. "She was sick last year. Her kidneys finally failed." After all the grief she'd endured, Gertrude's death had just about overwhelmed her, and she hadn't been able to think about getting herself another dog, though Stephen had begged her to reconsider. In fact, she had the distinct impression he was going to choose a pup from the abbey kennel as a present for her.

"Fabrice can stay with you tonight," he muttered, "but tomorrow night he'll sleep with the others. He has to learn discipline at this stage or he'll be useless in the mountains."

"Tomorrow night?" she repeated, instantly alert.

"A major storm front has moved in and I doubt it'll let up for two or three days." On that note, he briskly extinguished the oil lamp, cloaking the interior of the hut in darkness except for the flickering glow cast by the dying fire on the stone walls. Emma nestled beneath the covers and Raoul lay on his side, facing away from her.

Two or three days! She felt a rush of guilt at the up-heaval she was doubtless causing at the abbey. Poor Stephen. Yet she was defiantly grateful that the elements were cooperating. This would probably be her only chance to learn the truth from Raoul. She'd wanted to track him to his lair where she'd have him all to herself. It seemed she'd been granted her wish, two years too late. The Raoul she'd known had changed beyond comprehension and she had no idea how to reach the enigmatic man he'd become.

Now that all was quiet, questions chased around and around her mind. When did he say his prayers or whatever it was a priest had to do? Did her presence prevent him from carrying out his religious duties? Again she felt remorse over her rash decision to follow him up here on the mountain. So many lives had been disturbed because of her obsessive search.

Ten minutes later she was still awake and knew exactly why. Hoping Raoul had gone to sleep, she slid from the cot and stepped into her ski boots, which had been placed near the fire. Fabrice accompanied her. The other dogs raised their heads and made low noises at the slight disturbance.

She heard Raoul's sharp intake of breath. "What are you doing out of bed?" He sat up in the bag, fully clothed like Emma.

Moistening her dry lips, she said, "I have to go outside for a minute."

Quickly he raised himself from the floor and lighted the lantern. "I thought you'd gone out earlier."

"I hadn't drunk any apple juice earlier. I'm sorry."

Without saying another word, he helped her on with her parka, then opened the door. Fabrice would have followed her outside if Raoul hadn't admonished him to stay put. Emma took care not to touch Raoul's fingers as he handed her the lantern.

Never in her life had she known a mountain blizzard such as this. The violence of the gale-force winds terrified her. After even a few minutes of the driving, howling snow, it was sheer bliss to rush back into the warmth and safety of the hut. Raoul took the lantern and closed the door while she rid herself of her ice-encrusted parka. It had formed that fast!

His brow furrowed. "Perhaps now you're aware of the danger you were courting on the glacier today."

Emma turned away from him so he wouldn't hear the chattering of her teeth as she leaned over to take off her boots.

Fabrice was right there to lick her hands. At least *he* seemed glad to see her and she got down on her knees to hug him.

When she finally let him go and stood up, she surprised a bleak, hunted look in Raoul's eyes before he extinguished the lantern. Maybe she'd imagined it, but a chill of a different kind crept over her body, reminding her that two years had changed Raoul beyond recognition. She was alone in a mountain hut with a stranger—a priest, furthermore, who had deliberately renounced the conjugal life. He must find this situation with Emma awkward, or worse.

"Good night," she whispered after crawling into bed. She was strangely reluctant to provoke his wrath again or invite his contempt. Tomorrow would be time enough to demand answers that had robbed her of two years of love and fulfillment, and the joy of having his child.

The dogs settled down when Raoul got into the sleeping bag. She experienced another wave of guilt when she realized her presence had consigned him to a cold, uncomfortable night on the floor. She alone was responsible for their untenable situation.

She drew some comfort from Fabrice's presence. The other dogs clustered around Raoul, but Fabrice took up his vigil at Emma's side and rested his head against her hand in an endearing gesture that brought tears to her eyes.

Outside it sounded like the end of the world. Trying to escape the ceaseless noise, she buried her head beneath the blanket. Raoul must have heard her restless stirring. "You're safe," came his deep voice out of the darkness. "Sleep now. You're going to need every ounce of strength before long."

Emma frowned. *What did he mean by that?*

CHAPTER FIVE

THANKS TO RAOUL'S ministrations, Emma awakened late the next day with a sense of well-being. She found to her surprise that he'd already prepared breakfast, built up the fire and gone outside with the dogs. The sleeping bag was back in the corner.

As he'd predicted, the storm had not yet abated, but Raoul obviously wasn't letting it interfere with his work of putting the dogs through maneuvers. Then again, maybe he needed privacy to say his daily prayers. Or maybe he was avoiding her. . . .

Quickly she donned her boots and parka and made a little trip outside. Nothing had changed from the night before. The storm was still venting its fury, and Emma could see nothing but the blinding whiteness all around. She wondered where Raoul had taken the dogs. She hurried back inside, seeking the fire's warmth.

After making her bed, Emma helped herself to the omelet and bread he'd left for her along with a thermos of hot chocolate. She ate everything, still troubled by his ominous remark of the night before.

He must have meant that as soon as the storm died down, he'd be taking her back to the abbey and wanted her to keep up her strength. No doubt he couldn't wait to be rid of her. But before that happened, she had to find a way to get through to him, persuade him to tell her the truth about his disappearance. *And then what?* Though she'd promised to leave him at the earliest possible moment, the thought of being separated from him again filled her with a new and unexpected kind of pain.

Unused to being idle, she washed the dishes with part of the hot water left in the saucepan on the camp stove. Then she took advantage of the privacy his absence afforded to sponge bathe with the rest. After that, she dressed in her ski clothes, which were reasonably dry after hanging by the fireplace all night.

She glanced around the room. There was nothing to do but put another log on the fire. She couldn't even brush her hair; fortunately, though, it was naturally curly. She ran her fingers through it, wishing there was a mirror in the hut.

But if Raoul had such things as a hairbrush, for instance, she didn't want to be caught looking for it. Once was enough. He'd left the oil lamp burning to give more light. Emma decided to risk his anger long enough to get a book she'd seen in one of the bags. Raoul might be gone for hours and she needed something to occupy her mind.

Settling for a mystery novel, she stretched out on the cot to read. At first the story absorbed her, but after several hours, she started worrying about Raoul and kept listening for him and the dogs. Her anxiety grew, and she finally slipped the book beneath her pillow and started pacing the floor. It seemed as though he'd been gone all day. Again she cursed the fact that she'd lost her watch because she had no idea of the time.

When her stomach started to complain, she realized it must be close to the dinner hour. Surely he should be back by now! Unable to stand it any longer, she began to prepare a meal with the provisions she could find, attempting to keep her fears for his safety at bay. When he returned, he'd be starving. She absolutely refused to listen to the little voice that said, "*If* he returned." Fate couldn't be that cruel.

The hut's makeshift kitchen contained an astonishing supply of dried and dehydrated foods. She decided to prepare beef goulash and stewed tomatoes with a dessert of dried apricots. The water for the coffee was beginning to boil when Raoul suddenly swept in with the dogs, covered head to foot in snow and ice. She could still hear the wind howling outside.

Before relieving himself of his own gear, he attended to the dog's needs and prepared their food, ignoring Emma as if she wasn't there. The feelings that welled up inside her were contradictory but equally intense. On the one hand, she was faint with relief that he'd returned safely. On the other, she was indignant at his indifference.

"Your dinner's ready."

"So I see." He reached for the mug of hot coffee she'd just poured.

Anger made her face go hot and she felt like dashing the contents in his face. "Have you lived in priestly silence so long you've forgotten how to say thank you, or even explain why you were out all day? Anything could have happened to you! I've worried myself sick!"

He avoided comment and patted the dogs' heads to soothe them before eating his goulash. Clearly they weren't used to hearing a woman's voice, let alone the strident tone of a infuriated woman fast losing control. She knew that was how she sounded to Raoul and determined to rein in her emotions so she could have a civilized talk with him.

As soon as she started to wash the dishes, he got down his parka. Emma couldn't believe it. "You're frightened to be alone with me, aren't you? I had no idea you were such a coward," she taunted, hoping for a reaction. "Only a dishonorable man would drag me through the farce of an engagement and wedding preparations with no intention of showing up for the ceremony. Is there a sadistic streak in you that derives pleasure from making me suffer?"

He flashed her a look of fury that under other circumstances would have frightened her, but right now she was too far gone to care. "And what about your mother? She's never been the same since. She exists, but you wouldn't call it living. As for Roger and Etienne, they worship you...." Her voice cracked. "Doesn't that mean anything to you?"

Raoul wheeled away from her, his complexion the color of paste. "What I did was for my reasons and mine alone!" he retorted over his shoulder. "And if I was faced with the same decision today, I'd handle it exactly the same way. Is that clear?"

"Perfectly!" Her eyes flashed blue sparks. "You're a poor excuse for a human being, Father John. Be assured I'll never tell anyone you're still alive. It would destroy our families to know what you've done, what you're capable of."

His head was bowed. Maybe he was praying. She had no idea what went on inside him, and at this point she didn't care. She felt numb, incapable of emotion. He'd killed the last particle of tenderness she felt for him.

"The minute the storm breaks, I'll go back to the abbey. All you need to do is point me in the right direction." She'd seen the mountaineering gear kept in the hut and knew how to use it. He'd taught her how to climb and rappel. Besides, getting back to the abbey on her own couldn't possibly be as dangerous as traversing that glacier. There had to be a trail, otherwise the dogs wouldn't be here with Raoul.

"You'd never make it to the abbey without help, so put that idea out of your mind," he ground out with a ferocity that stunned her as he pulled on his gloves.

"Don't you dare dictate to me," she retorted heatedly. "I made it up here alone. Surely the route you and the dogs used isn't comparable to my trek to the hut."

He stood by the door with his legs apart, hands on his hips, looking like an avenging angel. "You made it across that ice field by the grace of God, Emma."

"Let's take that a little further, shall we? In His infinite mercy, He allowed me to reach you so my pain could end." She paused, closing her eyes. "Don't worry, Raoul," she went on, her voice scornful. "I'll tell everyone I found a cave to hide in until the blizzard passed out. No one will ever know we met or that I trespassed on your precious inner sanctum. Rest assured, your secret will go to the grave with me!"

A blackness seemed to fill the room when he left, banging the door behind him. This in turn disturbed the dogs who stared at Emma in bewilderment but were curiously silent, no doubt because they sensed the hostility between her and Raoul.

Emma stood by the hearth and absently stroked Fabrice's head, aware of nothing but a cold emptiness. She stared into the dying flames, all the strength gone out of her. She barely had the energy to crawl into bed fully clothed. Fabrice followed at her heels and rested his head and paw next to her pillow. She hugged him around the neck for comfort.

Raoul had changed so totally from the man she once knew, it was almost as if another spirit inhabited his body. The transformation actually frightened her, because she could find no way to communicate with him, no access.

He returned a few minutes later and commanded Fabrice to join the other dogs, but Fabrice hesitated.

Raoul immediately chastised him and dragged him away from Emma's bedside.

Raoul's actions reminded her of another time, when he'd physically removed Gertrude from the room so he could be completely alone with Emma. Then, the look of naked longing in his eyes had made her forget everything but the need to be in his arms.

But that was part of the distant past. Right now his eyes were like chips of black ice. He had no feelings for her and intended to squelch Fabrice's affection, as well. Not wanting to watch or hear him discipline the dog, she buried her head beneath the pillow.

When everything grew quiet she lifted her head to look over at Raoul. He lay on his side with his back toward her, propped up on one elbow. She blinked as she saw him put something in his mouth, then drink from the cup he'd used at dinner.

Was he ill? Did he have a headache? More than anything in the world Emma wanted to ask him what was wrong but knew he'd refuse to answer.

She laid her head back on the pillow. When she'd known Raoul, he had never suffered from headaches. In fact, he'd always been remarkably healthy. But anything could have happened to him in the intervening two years.

Her thoughts returned to her conversations with Lorna about possible reasons for Raoul's disappearance. Now, the idea that he might be terminally ill didn't sound so farfetched. Maybe he had a disease that was slowly draining him. Knowing Raoul, he would fight it to the bitter end and never let on. What better place to end his days than among the monks of the abbey?

Suddenly she remembered Father André's warning not to go up on the lift. By now the priests would know she was missing and consider it their duty to search for her. She berated herself again for her recklessness. In her single-minded compulsion to reach Raoul, she hadn't given the others a thought. Only now did she really understand the gravity of what she'd done.

Hot tears trickled out of the corners of her eyes before she fell into a troubled sleep, wishing the other priests didn't have to pay for her impetuosity. In her anguish and aloneness, she missed the closeness of the young Saint Bernard who'd attached himself to her in an amazingly short period of time.

The next day was a repeat of the one before. Upon awakening, Emma discovered that Raoul had already rolled up his bag and gone outside with the dogs, leaving breakfast made for her. With nothing to do and the storm even worse, she had no choice but to entertain herself; she'd read two novels by the time Raoul and the dogs came in for dinner.

No words passed between them as they ate their simple meal of soup and crackers. The silence continued while he settled the dogs and prepared himself for bed. Emma climbed into the cot after dinner and pulled the covers over her head, hating the enforced quiet. Fabrice had apparently learned his lesson and didn't try to approach her that night. She supposed he, too, could sense his master's ominous mood and wasn't willing to risk another rebuke.

Though she pretended to be asleep while Raoul got ready for bed, she peeked out from under the pillow in time to catch him taking another pill. Her anxiety for his welfare increased; the very real possibility that he was dying from a terminal illness of some kind filled her with dread. She didn't think she could bear to remain in ignorance much longer.

At some point she did fall asleep, but it was fitful, and toward morning something disturbed her, waking her fully. Maybe it was a whimper from one of the dogs. She sat up in bed, glancing automatically at the hearth where Raoul slept. In the faint glow from the fire she could see that his sleeping bag was still there, but he wasn't in it. Evidently he'd had to go outside.

She listened for his return, but after a few minutes she started to grow anxious. What if he was too sick to make it back inside the hut without help? Alarmed by the thought, she threw off the covers and hurried to the door. Except for the wind, everything seemed quiet outside. Apparently the storm was abating.

Her eyes swept over the room once more, and quite by accident she noticed a pair of snowshoes missing and—she was almost sure of it—a length of climbing rope. Her gaze shot to the corner where only one pair of skis remained. *Hers*.

Looking carefully around now, she could see he'd left out extra rations of food and water for the dogs.

Emma's heart began to thud. *He had disappeared again!*

Maybe he'd gone to recover the radio. But in her heart of hearts, she feared that now the weather was better, he'd headed back to the abbey, hoping to reach the priests before they began a fruitless search. She knew he'd send another priest to take care of her and the dogs and get her back to safety. But before that could happen, he would be long gone from the abbey. His stealth in escaping without waking her, without telling her his intentions, was the last straw.

Once again his sudden disappearance brought back the horror of the past. She wasn't about to let him do that twice! Especially not when she knew he could be ill. Although she was becoming reconciled to the fact that he was a monk, she wasn't going to let him go through this agony alone. She was a doctor and could help him.

And if he wasn't ill? Then all she wanted was a chance to see him one last time and say goodbye.

The dogs settled down again, except for Fabrice who stood by the door, alert, eyeing her with uncanny compassion, as if he sensed Raoul had deserted them both.

Right or wrong didn't enter into it any longer. She had to follow him! Fabrice would guide her. Finding a victim in the vast frozen wilderness was what he'd been trained to do and he knew Raoul's scent better than anyone's.

He couldn't have been gone very long because the logs he'd added to the fire hadn't yet had a chance to burn down. Not wasting another minute, Emma threw on her gear and put rations for both her and Fabrice, along with the binoculars, into a backpack she found hanging on the wall. Quickly she reached for a pair of snowshoes, which she fastened to the top of the pack. Then she pulled one of Raoul's heavy sweaters from his duffel bag.

"Fabrice," she called to the dog who immediately padded over to her. She knelt on the floor and held Raoul's sweater to his muzzle, forcing him to smell it. "Find Father John. Please, Fabrice." Tears filled her eyes as she hugged the dog tightly. "I think he's gone back to the abbey. Do you understand? The abbey! Help me find Father John. If he gets away from me now, I'll never see him again. He's ill. I know he is," she whispered brokenly.

He ambled toward the door panting excitedly and waving his tail in anticipation. The other dogs were alert by now and they got to their feet, sensing that something wasn't right. Emma commanded them to lie down again, and after a brief moment, they obeyed.

Quickly Emma pulled on her ski mask, then put on the heavy backpack. Once that was accomplished, she retrieved her skis and poles, hoisted them over her shoulder and left the hut with Fabrice in the lead. They made their way through the narrow opening to the rocks, which served as steps to the frozen glacier below. Fabrice knew the path and guided Emma down the face with the confident expertise of a true mountaineer.

Morning was making its appearance, heralded by the lavender-gray tinge on the clouds to the east. The snow had stopped falling, but the wind was still gusting at perhaps twenty miles an hour. Already the drifting snow had covered Raoul's tracks, but Fabrice seemed to know exactly where to go and barked excitedly.

As fast as she could, Emma put on the snowshoes and they were off. Once again—as she had that first day—Emma felt impervious to the elements. She concentrated on finding a rhythm for picking up and setting down the shoes to give her the fastest speed. She hadn't come this far in her quest only to lose Raoul now. She trudged on, placing her faith in the courageous Saint Bernard.

They hadn't been traveling more than ten minutes when she realized Fabrice was leading her in a northeasterly direction, away from the abbey far below. When she stood on a snowy crag, she could just make out the gray structure through the binoculars.

"Fabrice, we're going the wrong way. Find Father John."

He barked as if he understood, but persisted in heading away from the monastery, turning his head every so often to see if she was following.

Emma didn't know what to think and was afraid to go any farther, her mind in a quandary. Fabrice was an intelligent dog. Raoul wouldn't have been training him on the mountain if he weren't the pick of the litter. Yet the dog was going cross-country, leading her deeper and deeper into the Sawatch Mountains.

She was on the verge of turning back to the hut when Fabrice ran up to her and caught the edge of her parka sleeve between his teeth, tugging gently. He acted as if he knew exactly what he was doing. She stared into his beautiful, solemn eyes. He was clearly trying to communicate something to her.

In that instant, Emma decided she had to trust him. Maybe something had already happened to Raoul. Maybe he was unconscious or had unwittingly wandered away from the established route back to the abbey. Visions of his body lying frozen at the bottom of a fissure gave impetus to her fear, and she followed blindly in Fabrice's tracks. Her only thought was to find Raoul. If he was in danger, he had no dogs with him to go for help.

Emma paused frequently to eat some hard tack and to rest. Each time before continuing she tried to find Raoul with the aid of her binoculars, but to her dismay she never saw anything except snow, swept up by the gusting winds. She shifted her skis to her other shoulder and trudged on.

Judging by the sun's position above the fast-moving clouds, they'd been going for at least three hours. There was still no sign of Raoul and Emma began to feel really afraid. Anything could have happened to him.

She stopped again, exhausted because she was un-used to snowshoes. Not once had Fabrice faltered. It was as though he possessed built-in radar that seemed to be locked on an unknown target.

They rested for about twenty minutes, ate some of their rations and drank a little water before moving on. A half hour or so later, when Emma thought she couldn't take another step, she came upon a sight that took her breath away. In fact, she recognized it from the photograph hanging on the museum wall at the abbey. Laid out beneath a deep blanket of snow was Holy Cross City. The ghost town lay hidden in a kind of bowl surrounded by mountain peaks.

She and Stephen had read about it as they browsed in the library before dinner on their second night at the abbey. A thriving mining camp in the late 1800s, it had long since been deserted, but parts of the original structures remained standing.

"Good dog," Emma praised Fabrice. She was al-most certain he'd truly picked up Raoul's scent. But why in the name of heaven had Raoul come to this place? For what possible reason?

Convinced they were close to finding him and ea-ger to set a faster pace, she replaced the cumbersome snowshoes with skis. After fastening the shoes to the top of her pack, she pushed off behind Fabrice who was acting more and more excited. Raoul couldn't be far away if the dog's behavior was anything to go by.

There were few rocks or trees to impede her prog-ress as they drew closer to the random cluster of dilapidated wooden shacks that had once been Holy Cross City. Her heart began to hammer as she mentally braced herself for Raoul's anger when he discovered she'd followed him—or for something worse. An ill or injured Raoul, perhaps....

Because she was so intent on her thoughts, she didn't notice that Fabrice had come to an abrupt stop and was skirting something in the snow.

She tried to slow down, but she'd reacted too late. The momentum from the last thrust kept her skis gliding. In a heroic effort, Fabrice hurled himself into her path, but he still couldn't prevent her from dropping into a dark hole.

In an instant, her whole life seemed to flash before her. *"Raoul!"* she screamed in terror.

CHAPTER SIX

THE PLUNGE KNOCKED the wind out of her, and for a minute she saw stars. Throughout the ordeal Fabrice barked wildly.

When her eyes could focus, she realized she'd fallen about ten feet and landed on her pack. She could see the dog, who'd crept to the edge of what appeared to be the opening of an abandoned mine shaft. She tried to get up, but her left ankle felt as if it were on fire. The agonizing pain shot up through her body and she almost fainted.

She cried out, clutching her injured leg. The fall had snapped her ski; part of it was still in the binding. Her other ski had come off and was lying somewhere, probably on the surface, with her poles. She'd obviously broken her ankle, but when she considered everything, she recognized that this was another miracle—that once again her life had been spared.

Quickly she pulled off her ski mask. "Fabrice!" she shouted. "Go find Father John. Get Father John!" she begged the dog who barked loudly before turning away from the opening. The fact that he left her without question led her to believe that Raoul was nearby and the dog knew where to find him.

The cold inside the shaft had quickly penetrated to her bones, and she realized hypothermia was her greatest enemy at the moment. She didn't want to be any more of a burden to Raoul, but she had no choice. She had to rely on him to rescue her. Again. She could only hope he himself didn't need rescuing....

Biting her lip, she removed the straps of her pack, then turned on her side in an effort to release her injured foot from the ski binding. After several clumsy attempts she managed it. She lay there crazed with an excruciating pain that soaked her in perspiration and left her weak and trembling.

She waited until the nausea passed, then tried to get up on her right foot to see if she could do anything to help herself out of the shaft. But the slightest movement made her ankle throb so badly she had to take deep, controlled breaths to keep from screaming. It was broken all right. She must have passed out from the pain, because the next thing she was aware of was Fabrice's frantic barking.

"Emma?" Raoul's frantic voice called to her from a distance. The sound of his voice caused the tears to gush from her eyes and she sent up a silent prayer of thanks.

"Raoul! I've fallen in a shaft. Please be careful!" she cried, so overjoyed Fabrice had found him she momentarily forgot her pain and raised herself to a sitting position.

Suddenly she was blinking at a broad swath of light as he trained his powerful flashlight on her from the edge. *"Mon Dieu,"* he murmured on a shuddering breath. The emotion she heard in his voice told her he cared. "How badly are you hurt?"

"M-my ankle's broken, but other than that I'm f-fine," she answered with difficulty. Her body was shivering from the cold and her lips were too stiff to form words very well.

"Don't move. I'm coming down for you," he said in an authoritative voice that told her he was in charge despite whatever was wrong with him physically. Again her impulsive decision to track him here had forced him to put his life in danger. Shame washed over her in waves.

"I—I'm sorry I've caused you more grief when it's obvious you wanted to get away from me. It would serve me right if you left me here to d-die."

"Stop talking rubbish," he muttered as he worked quickly and expertly to lower himself by rope. Within minutes he reached her and before she knew what was happening, he inserted a pill in her mouth, then put a cup of water to her lips. "Drink, Emma. This will dull the pain." Because he carried strong painkillers, she was more than ever convinced he had something seriously wrong with him.

She had difficulty swallowing but she was too thankful to have found Raoul again to complain. One hand held the back of her head while the other steadied the cup.

"Lie still and try to relax while I fashion a splint. I know you're freezing, but I have to secure your ankle before I can take you out of here."

For the next little while Emma lay there, clamping down on the pain as Raoul proceeded to work. He focused the flashlight on her leg and slit her pant leg and ski underwear up to her thigh. When he removed her boot and then her sock, she cried out in agony.

"I know it hurts. Be brave a little longer. I'll be through here in a minute. You must have a guardian angel, because there's no broken skin, no dislocation, that I can see. Only the normal amount of swelling. I think an X ray will reveal a clean fracture."

It must have been because of his many years of experience as a world-class skier that he knew exactly how to apply the splint and wrap it. Emma groaned several times, but finally the ordeal was over. He pulled her insulated stocking over her foot as far as it would stretch.

"Now," he said, getting to his feet, "I'm going to pick you up and carry you over my shoulder. Do everything I say, and we can keep your discomfort to a minimum. Ready?"

"Y-yes."

"Bon." With a strength and agility she could scarcely believe, he grasped her by the waist and hoisted her over his broad shoulder, taking the utmost care not to disturb her leg more than necessary.

The pill he'd given her must have been extremely powerful. Although she was still uncomfortable, the devouring flame in her ankle seemed to have diminished. Feeling light-headed, she was hardly aware of Raoul's climb up the rope and the trek through the snow, with Fabrice leading the way. All she knew was that Raoul was carrying her in his arms—the only place she wanted to be. Right now, it was difficult to remember why that was wrong....

They approached a dilapidated shack on the outskirts of the ghost town whose roof looked ready to cave in from the snow. Nevertheless, Raoul seemed to have no qualms about entering it. She gazed around the small, square room with its rough plank flooring. The windows were boarded up to keep out the worst of the elements. As for the interior, it was empty except for Raoul's backpack, along with a few other bags, a small camp stove in one corner, a supply of wood, and an unmade cot near the hearth. That was where he placed her.

Though Raoul had started a fire before rescuing her, the heat hadn't begun to relieve the bitter cold of the room. He added more logs, then drew some wool blankets from a bag against the wall. Quickly and efficiently, he pulled off her other ski boot and covered her shivering body from head to toe with the blankets.

Emma was aware of Fabrice's padding around her cot, but Raoul didn't appear to notice the dog's presence. His attention was fastened on Emma. "How's the ankle now?" he asked, hovering over her anxiously.

"N-not nearly as bad," she hastened to reassure him. "That s-splint has made all the difference. I—I'm sure I couldn't have done it any b-better." Lifting her head she asked, "Are you all r-right, Raoul?"

He gave her a startled look. "Why do you ask that?"

"Because I know you're i-ill. I've seen you taking p-pills when you didn't know I was watching. I'm a doctor. I can read the s-signs. You're in pain."

"Don't be absurd. I get the occasional headache like everyone else."

"No. It's m-more than that. Otherwise you'd have gone down to the abbey. I want to help you. Please let me. That's why I...followed you here, so you wouldn't have to go through it alone."

"Right now we have to concentrate on your needs," he retorted as if he hadn't heard anything she'd said.

It didn't surprise her. She lay there weak and helpless, but above all grateful she hadn't completely lost him. "How is Fabrice? He was so wonderful."

"He was indeed," Raoul said. "As soon as you fell through the opening of that old mine shaft, he sniffed me out and practically dragged me there. His only instinct was to save your life. They don't come any better than Fabrice."

Emma called softly to the dog, who stood nearby and licked her outstretched hand. "Thank you, Fabrice. What would I have done without you?" The dog seemed to understand and cocked his head.

Raoul's dark brows met in a frown. "You're frozen, Emma. Even though you weren't down there very long, it was enough to lower your body temperature. It's going to take time for this shack to heat up enough to give you the warmth you need. Fabrice can speed up the process."

At Raoul's command, the dog plopped his head on Emma's chest, seeming to understand the situation with the uncanny instincts of his breed. On a low moan he tried to get as close to her as possible while she wrapped her arms around his neck. It was amazing how much warmth the dog exuded. How much love...

"Oh, Fabrice..." She sobbed quietly into his fur as her eyes began to close.

THE NEXT TIME she was aware of her surroundings, she discovered her parka had been removed and she was alone in the cot, with the blankets tucked beneath her chin as though she were a child. Her throbbing ankle was nothing compared to her sudden fear that once again Raoul had disappeared without a trace.

"Raoul?" she screamed in panic. With difficulty she raised herself onto one elbow. Her movement caused Fabrice to lift his head from her hip and whimper.

Except for flickers of firelight dancing over the walls and ceiling, the interior of the shack was shrouded in darkness. At last the roaring blaze was throwing out enough heat to counteract the extreme cold.

"I'm right here, Emma." Raoul emerged from the shadows behind her dressed in his sweater and ski pants, carrying a cup. His dark eyes narrowed worriedly on her face as he sat on the edge of the cot opposite Fabrice. "Take this pill, then I'll give you dinner."

He helped her to sit up while she swallowed the pill and drank thirstily, draining every drop of water.

"I'm sorry," she said when she'd finished. "I didn't mean to cry out like that but I was afraid you'd gone again."

She heard him mutter something before he got to his feet, and she thought she detected a flash of pain in his eyes. "Do you honestly think I'd leave you alone in your condition?" There was a long pause. "Stay under the covers," he admonished. Then he went to the camp stove in the corner to get a steaming cup of coffee, its rich aroma filling the room. He again helped her to a sitting position to drink.

"This will warm you. And while you're sipping it, I'll fix us some stew and crackers. We're out of bread."

Emma took several swallows of the scalding liquid, feeling more restored by the second. "There's bread and food for us and Fabrice in my backpack."

He eyed her pensively. "It's already night and too late to go out. In the morning I'll return to the shaft. Right now my only concern is that you're well fed and warm. Fabrice can eat some of the stew. How's your ankle?"

While he spoke, he draped another blanket around her back and shoulders. Emma was far too aware of his touch, but tried to hide her reaction. She had to keep reminding herself that he was Father John, that he'd taken holy orders—which included a vow of chastity. She knew he'd look after anyone else with the same degree of caring and dedication.

"It's fine, thanks to you."

"Don't lie to me, Emma. I want to know your exact condition."

She lifted her head. "Naturally it hurts, but the medicine is very effective and I'm feeling much more myself. In fact, I'm getting hot, though when you brought me here, I didn't think I'd ever be warm again." She took a deep breath. "Thank you."

His brief nod told her he was satisfied with her response. He brought her a plate of stew.

"At least now your teeth aren't chattering when you talk. When you go back to sleep for the night, I'll elevate your leg to keep down the swelling. While you're eating, I'll feed Fabrice and take him outside before we all bed down for the night."

Emma nodded, following his movements as she ate her dinner, although it seemed to lodge in her throat. The mere thought of spending another night under the same roof with Raoul was proving too much for her chaotic emotions.

He could have no idea of her deep-seated longings, or of the fact that she was aware of him in all the old ways. What frightened her most was that she wouldn't be able to go on hiding those feelings or the needs he aroused in her without even trying.

Shame consumed her at these thoughts, and she forced herself to remember that Raoul no longer felt desire for her or any woman. He'd repudiated her when he took his vows. As long as he didn't know she was burning inside for him, it would be all right. *It had to be!*

Raoul's low command to Fabrice reached her ears, and seconds later she heard the door open and close. The wind was still gusting outside. She shivered, but this time it wasn't with cold. It was with a kind of excitement—a forbidden excitement as she anticipated the moment when Raoul would lie in front of the fire where she could see him. She bit the underside of her lip to stem the tide of yearning that made every part of her come alive. If only she could fall asleep before Raoul came back!

But Fabrice wanted to return to the warmth of the hut too quickly for that to happen. She heard the sound of logs being put on the fire, then felt the bottom of the blanket being lifted so Raoul could prop up her injured leg.

Once he was satisfied she'd be comfortable, he stood by the cot and ate his dinner from the pot he'd used to heat the stew. All the while he focused his attention on the hearth. Unaccountably disturbed by the haunted expression in his eyes as he stared into the flames, she avoided looking at him and huddled beneath the blankets.

A few minutes later he whispered, "Are you all right? Can I get you anything else before we go to sleep?"

Yes, she mused inwardly. *There's something you can do for me,* she wanted to confess. Instead she pressed her knuckles against her lips. "I'm fine now. Honestly. You've taken such wonderful care of me. I don't deserve it." She paused, then said deliberately, "Thank you, Father John." That was now his name, after all. She'd been forced to come to terms with his new identity. She wanted to honor it, for his sake.

"Don't say that!" The harshness in his tone caught her off guard and she closed her eyes tightly.

"I'm sorry. I didn't mean to offend you. I don't know what to say or how to act in front of you. I've never known a priest before. Please forgive me for calling you Raoul all this time."

She could feel the tensile strength of his powerful body. "Stop asking my forgiveness."

Her cheeks grew hot. "I know I'm a burden you can't wait to be rid of, yet in the last few days, you've saved my life twice. I wouldn't be human if I weren't grateful. You were always a remarkable man, but you make an even more remarkable priest. To be honest, I'm very much in awe of you." *And in love. That would never change—even if* he *had.*

She heard him mutter something in French before he rasped, "I'm no saint, Emma! I'm made of the same flesh and blood as you."

"I realize that, but you can't deny the fact that some extraordinary quality in you compelled you to take vows. It's obvious you don't want my gratitude, but you have it all the same."

After a long silence he said, "Gratitude is the last emotion you should be feeling toward me." The self-deprecation in his voice tore at her.

"What's happened to this point is in the past," she told him honestly. "I intruded on your world, uninvited, and among my many sins, I forced you to put your life in jeopardy to save mine. For what it's worth, I'm ashamed of my behavior. You spoke the truth when you accused me of being impetuous. It's an ugly trait. One I'm going to try to change."

"If I hadn't provoked you to the point of madness, you wouldn't have felt the need to track me all the way up the mountain, risking your life a hundred times over. I'm to blame for your broken ankle and much, much more."

Emma's remorse deepened. "Please don't say that. I can see why you broke things off the way you did two years ago. If you'd told me you couldn't go through with our marriage because you wanted to be a priest, I'd have fallen apart. We both know it's true. I couldn't have tolerated any reason that kept you from me. What you did was for the best. I don't blame you for anything," she whispered.

"After what I've caused you to suffer, how can you say that?" His tortured query surprised her.

"None of it matters anymore. All I care about is that I found you, that you're alive and that, despite the pain you have to endure, whatever it is, you've found peace at the abbey. It's enough."

"You think I'm at peace?"

The torment in his voice was so real Emma forgot about her leg and eased onto her back so she could look at him. The motion started a new throbbing in her ankle, but she was scarcely aware of it as she studied him. Even by firelight she could discern the anguish in his eyes. "Aren't you?" she asked incredulously.

"Mon Dieu, Emma!" His voice shook. "I've forgotten the meaning of the word, and being with you again—" He broke off, then swallowed with difficulty. "A man can only take so much."

"What are you saying?" Emma couldn't catch her breath. But staring into his black eyes, she had her answer, and if she hadn't already been lying down, she would've fallen. That old familiar look of desire was there, burning for her, letting her know he wanted her. A person could pretend many things, but desire leapt to life of its own accord. She began to feel afraid and turned her head away.

"So now you know," he said in a husky voice that sent more shock waves through her body. "And there's no place to run."

Hadn't she said the same thing when she'd followed him onto the mountain? Her thoughts came back to mock her now. "It's because I've placed us in an impossible position, and you did what had to be done to save my life. That's all. A priest is human." Her voice quavered, despite her best intentions. She was not prepared for his next words.

"I'm not a priest."

CHAPTER SEVEN

THE SILENCE THAT FOLLOWED his statement confused her further. "Please don't talk that way. You don't know what you're saying. You're—you're exhausted from lack of sleep and taking care of me. Our situation would try the patience of a saint."

She hoped he'd move farther away, but to her dismay he stayed right where he was, bigger than life. She closed her eyes in an attempt to shut him out.

"I'm not Father John," Raoul persisted. "I wear no cross, no ring."

"Don't lie to me," she begged, fighting herself, as well as him. She'd been wrong to pursue Raoul, but she refused to be the reason he broke one of his vows. That sin would weigh too heavily on her conscience. "You're a priest!"

"I'm Raoul Villard. Nothing more, nothing less. What will it take to convince you of that?"

"I'm trying to prevent us from making a mistake we'll both regret."

"Emma?" he cried, sounding as if he couldn't take much more. "How can I make you believe me?"

She moistened her dry lips and tried to focus on him. "Earlier you told me Raoul Villard was dead, that there was only Father John,'' she said in a faintly accusing tone.

His hands curled into fists at his sides and his eyes fused with hers. ''I swear I've never taken vows. I'm not professed. I've never had a vocation for the priesthood and I never intend to have one. Thanks to the kindness and generosity of Abbot Emmanuel, the abbey has been my temporary home for the past few months.''

Emma stared hard at him, trying to make sense of what he was telling her, but the painkiller had dulled her senses and she couldn't concentrate. ''How do you expect me to believe you when I found you at the monastery?'' she asked finally. ''All the priests addressed you as Father John. You've made your home there. You work with the dogs. You were one of the priests who rescued us in the storm.'' She pulled the covers to her chin for protection. ''You worry me when you talk like this.''

''Worrying you is the last thing I want to do,'' he said huskily. *''Mignonne—''* the old endearment slipped out ''—it's been two years. A lifetime.''

The longing in his tone was real enough, but she was beginning to feel distanced from him. The powerful drug had robbed her of coherence. ''If you're not…a priest, what are you doing here?''

A long silence ensued. ''I've already told you more than I should have.''

Emma sighed heavily. "You always speak in riddles. I'm too tired to understand right now. Good night."

"Good night," he whispered. Maybe she dreamed that his fingers made soothing strokes through the curls at her temples.

There was no way to gauge the passage of time, but Emma thought it must be dawn when she finally awoke, needing to go outside. The fire had started to burn down, and Fabrice and Raoul were sound asleep in front of it. She hated the idea of disturbing him after all he'd been forced to suffer because of her.

For a few minutes she sat up in the cot, contemplating how to maneuver without waking them or further injuring her ankle. Finally she rolled onto her stomach and used the knee of her good leg to lever herself off the bed. All she had to do was hop as far as the door and then she'd have some support, but the effects of the pill lingered, making her unsteady.

To her chagrin, Fabrice's radar picked up the sound of her movements and he whined anxiously before trotting over to her, which alerted Raoul. When he saw her trying to balance on one leg, he jumped to his feet.

In an instant he reached for her parka and crossed the room to help her into it. "Why didn't you call me if you needed to go outside?"

"Because you've had to do too much for me already," she said as he forced her to sit down on the cot. After sliding a ski boot onto her uninjured foot, he picked her up in his arms and carried her to the door. Once he'd deposited her outside, he told her to knock when she was ready to come back in. Since his attitude remained impersonal, it made the whole situation easier to handle.

Fortunately for Emma, the weather was cooperating. Though the wind still gusted, the storm had definitely ended. Rays of apricot and rose streaked the sky. After the tempest they'd survived, Emma was filled with wonder at the beauty of the winter landscape. Soon the sun would be up. *And then what?*

She shivered. Last night Raoul had told her he wasn't a priest. He'd looked at her the way he used to. Even if she'd wanted to believe him, she'd been too drugged to respond. Without the medication, she'd probably have given in to the temptation to love him and would've awakened this morning filled with guilt because he'd broken his vows. And even greater anguish because she could never be his wife, never live with him

The bitterly cold air seemed to clear her head, and she knew now what she had to do. Determinedly, she knocked on the door. Raoul was right there to gather her in his arms once more and carry her back to the cot, using his foot to kick the door shut behind them.

Without speaking, he set her down gently on the mattress and proceeded to help her off with her parka and boot. Fabrice immediately laid his head by her shoulder and she patted him affectionately.

"It's going to be a beautiful day," she said, breaking the uneasy silence. "I'm feeling good enough for you to go back to the abbey and get help. I'll be fine here alone. Take Fabrice with you. I know you're anxious to get on with your duties.''

For a brief moment his face tightened, as if he was in the throes of turmoil. When he finally raised his head and their eyes met, his blazed like hot coals in the firelight and her heart started to thud heavily in her chest.

''I told you last night, Emma, I'm not a priest. And I've spent most of my time in the hut, not the abbey. So there's no reason for me to return there now. It's still early. Try to fall asleep again while I go for your pack.''

Summoning the dog, he put on his parka and reached for his climbing gear. They went outside, leaving Emma with her thoughts reeling. His quiet but firm declaration sounded like the Raoul she'd once known, a man whose sincerity was never in question. If he truly wasn't a priest, then what did all this mean?

One by one, she recalled little things she'd observed that had raised questions at the time, questions she'd somehow always explained away. But putting all these isolated incidents together, Emma could see a very different picture emerging and instinctively knew he'd been telling the truth. Pure revelation flowed through her and she sat up in the bed. *He wasn't a priest!*

What had Raoul said? He'd been allowed to stay at the monastery because of the goodness of the abbot? She could hardly take it in. Obviously when he'd left her and the dogs at the hut, he hadn't intended to go back to the abbey. But what did he hope to accomplish here in the mountains? Had Fabrice been to this shack with Raoul before? Was that why he knew where to lead Emma?

Evidently her arrival with Stephen had forced Raoul to flee the abbey, and that fact was torturing her now. He'd chosen one of the most remote spots on earth so no one would find him and disguised himself as a priest for protection. No wonder her presence in the kennel had been such a shock!

Emma found herself having to go through a complete thought reversal. These past few days she'd believed him to be a monk who'd given up the world to serve God. In reality, he'd been someplace else, doing something else, for most of the past two years. According to what he'd said earlier, he'd come to the abbey only a few months ago. Where had he been before that? Had he been sick at the time of their wedding, or was his illness more recent? Was that the reason he'd hidden in Colorado instead of returning to his family home in Montreal?

Then again, maybe he wasn't sick at all. Perhaps he'd taken the pills for a headache, just as he'd claimed. Emma frowned at the direction of her thoughts, which grew blacker as something equally insupportable crossed her mind.

Though she was elated he wasn't an ordained priest, in the past two years he could have become involved with another woman, could even have married her. On the heels of that thought came the daunting possibility that he might have been in love with another woman at the time of his impending marriage to Emma.

Maybe he'd been seeing someone else throughout their sporadic courtship—another champion skier perhaps, someone he couldn't give up—and at the last minute decided not to go through with the wedding.

Raoul would have had ample opportunity to carry on an affair without Emma's being aware of it, since there were many times he'd accepted invitations to conduct ski workshops at other resorts. Lorna had suggested as much, but Emma had been so confident of Raoul's love she'd never entertained the possibility. With hindsight, she conceded it would explain his disappearance, as well as his hostile attitude toward her since her arrival at the abbey.

If he was married, where was his wife? And what about last night? Was the desire he felt for Emma merely a temporary lapse, given the unusual circumstances? Now that it was morning, was Raoul relieved nothing had happened between them, after all? *Was there someone waiting for him?* If there'd been another woman all along, that might explain why he'd never taken Emma to bed.

Maybe he was on his way to this woman now. The mere thought caused the adrenaline to spurt once more. When she'd reconciled herself to the knowledge that he was a monk, she'd been content to leave things alone. But knowing he wasn't, knowing he'd

only been using the abbey to hide out, changed everything.

She could speculate all she wanted, but the fact remained that until she had answers to her questions
she'd never be at peace again!

Emma had to find some way to release her pent-up
energy and she managed to ease herself off the cot.
She hopped painfully to one corner of the shack and
reached for his ski poles, which she could use as
makeshift crutches. Luckily he'd left them behind and
had gone off on his snowshoes. Her skis and poles
were still at the mine shaft.

Before going out, Raoul had lighted the camp stove
to heat coffee. Right now she needed a stimulant to
fortify her and decided not to take any more painkillers. They were no longer necessary and only served to
dull her thinking.

It took some doing, but she finally succeeded in
pouring the strong black coffee into a mug. She took
a sip and felt an immediate surge of warmth. She was
swallowing the last drop just as Raoul swept into the
hut with her backpack and gear. He took off his parka
and gloves and laid them aside while Fabrice followed him around, obviously hungry.

Emma had had no warning of their approach, and
because everything was different now, his sudden
presence disarmed her. They were a man and a woman
with no barriers between them, except the ones Raoul
had chosen to erect. For the first time in three days she
was able to look at him and feast her eyes without

guilt. His dark male beauty took her breath away and always would.

"You shouldn't be up until that ankle's set in a cast," he cautioned as he emptied the backpack and prepared Fabrice's breakfast, darting Emma a piercing glance in the process.

She leaned heavily on the poles for balance. "You did such a good job of splinting it, I'm not sure it'll need one. Now that I know you're not a priest, I have to ask myself how you came to possess such expert medical knowledge. I realize you've probably seen a lot of injuries throughout your skiing career, but it still wouldn't account for the professional way you went about wrapping my ankle. If I didn't know better, I'd say you'd had training in the military as a medic."

He was busy feeding Fabrice and didn't acknowledge what she'd said, or even if he'd heard her. Suddenly something snapped inside Emma. Maybe it was because he'd ignored her once too often, she didn't know. But to her astonishment, tears sprang to her eyes and a sob escaped her throat. Everything had been dammed up inside her for too long.

Raoul must have heard her because he wheeled around abruptly. "Emma..." he groaned, crossing the space that separated them, taking her tearstained face in his hands. "I swore I wasn't going to let this happen," he muttered beneath his breath, but she heard him. Not understanding, she lifted drenched blue eyes to his. But he was already lowering his head and her eyelids fluttered closed as his mouth covered hers.

At the touch of his lips, the last two pain-filled years might never have been. Raoul was holding her, loving her again. Except for the added softness of his beard and mustache, his body felt the same. His mouth, his skin, everything tasted the same. If there was any change at all, it was that his hunger seemed greater than before, engulfing her in a mindless passion only Raoul had ever been capable of arousing.

His lips roved over her face and hair, then returned repeatedly to her mouth. She could taste the salt of her tears on his lips. As their kisses deepened, Emma was no longer aware of her surroundings and she tried to give him everything that had been denied them in the intervening years.

"Do you have any idea what you're doing to me?" His voice sounded hoarse, raw with emotion, as he kissed the tender skin of her neck and throat. "I shouldn't have started this, Emma," he admitted feverishly.

But Emma felt no such compunction. This was the man she loved, the man she needed. Obeying blind instinct, she melted against him and slid her arms around his back exactly the way she used to. Her action caused the ski poles to fall to the floor, but she was balanced on her good leg and didn't notice or care.

The only thing that mattered was to get close to him, so close nothing could ever part them again. As if they had a will of their own, her hands slid under his sweater and started to roam over his hard-muscled back, feeling the warmth of his skin.

"No, darling," he protested unexpectedly and tore his lips from hers. With a swiftness that left her breathless, he grasped her by the upper arms and held her away from him. But he'd reacted too late because she'd encountered something that had made her wince. Beneath her sensitive fingers she'd felt ridges of scar tissue running from one side of his back to the other beneath his shoulder blades.

Her voice shook. "What happened to you, Raoul? Please don't tell me it's nothing, because I'm a doctor and I know better."

His breathing grew shallow, as if he'd been running a great distance, and his black eyes seemed to look straight through her. "The accident that scarred my back happened two years ago. I won't lie to you about the pain. It was an experience I'd just as soon blot from my memory. But it's over and there's no discomfort at this point, so take that agonized look off your face."

Emma's pain increased. "No accident caused those lacerations. I felt how large and deep they are. Don't lie to me, Raoul. I've seen you taking pills and now I know why."

"Emma—" he shook her gently "—listen to me. When I tried to ease my way into the fissure the other day to get my radio, I scratched my back and it made the skin tender, so I took aspirin for a few nights."

"Next you'll say that being forced to carry me long distances under the worst kind of conditions, not once but twice, contributed nothing to your agony!" she cried in self-reproach.

"Stop it, Emma. You're torturing yourself for no reason."

She wanted to believe him and prayed he wasn't suffering, but something else was tearing her to pieces. "Then what's the real reason you stopped making love to me just now? Were you injured in other ways before the wedding? Is *that* why you didn't marry me? Because you don't think you're a whole man?" Her voice throbbed with anxiety. "Don't you know it would make no difference to me?" Scalding tears were running down her cheeks. "I love you so much—more than life itself!"

Her declaration reverberated throughout the shack, and Raoul's body tensed. From his pallor, she guessed he couldn't take much more. Without warning he picked her up in his arms and carried her the short distance to the cot.

Emma wrapped her arms around his neck and pressed her mouth to his, desperate to pour out her love to him, to show him nothing mattered as long as they were together. When he lowered her to the mattress she expected him to lie down with her and was alarmed when he forcibly removed her hands from the back of his neck.

Still clasping them, he stared down at her. "Whatever you're thinking, Emma, you'd be wrong." His voice sounded harsh and grating, as though he was in pain. "At this point I'm prepared to tell you everything."

She swallowed hard and clung to him. "Will it be the truth?"

His eyes met hers, and his voice rang with conviction. "There'll be no more lies, as God is my witness."

She had no choice but to believe him. Maybe it was because she'd always *wanted* to believe him. "So there have been lies, just as Lorna said."

After an interminable moment he said, "I was living a lie when I met you."

She'd wanted the truth, but now that she was hearing it from his lips, she was almost afraid of it and pulled her hands away. He reluctantly let them go as she sank back against the mattress, feeling inexplicably defeated and betrayed. Avoiding his eyes, she said dully, "Our whole relationship was a joke from start to finish, wasn't it? You never had any intention of marrying me."

He rubbed the back of his neck in a gesture that bespoke the intensity of his emotions. "On the morning of our wedding, I was en route to the church when I was forced off the road and kidnapped."

"*Kidnapped* . . ." Immediately she raised herself to a sitting position, staring at him incredulously.

"That's right. And until six months ago I was rotting away in a prison cell somewhere in Colombia."

Her first reaction was to accuse him of telling the most colossal lie of all, until she remembered the scars on his back. Aghast, she said, "You were beaten!"

Raoul nodded. "The usual form of torture. I was lucky. Some of the poor devils in there with me didn't make it out alive."

She shook her head, utterly stunned. "Why were you kidnapped? What would a South American hit squad want with a skier?"

"Skiing has always been a convenient cover for my real work."

"What real work?"

He pinned her with his dark gaze. "I learned how to splint a broken ankle like yours as part of my training with the RCMP."

She blinked. "Are you a doctor of some kind? Is that what those initials stand for?"

He made a strange noise in his throat. "I shouldn't be surprised. The States and Canada coexist but we truly don't know that much about each other. RCMP stands for the Royal Canadian Mounted Police."

Of course. Now that she thought about it, she remembered seeing those initials on a van when she'd arrived at the airport in Montreal. It took time for his words to sink in. "You're a *Mountie?*" she finally blurted out. "Like Sergeant Preston of the Yukon?"

Raoul frowned. "Who's Sergeant Preston?"

His bewildered expression made her smile. "He was the intrepid hero in a TV series from the fifties. Do you still ride horses and wear those fabulous red jack-

ets and Smokey the Bear hats? You'd look spectacu-
lar in an outfit like that, Raoul!''

He actually laughed out loud. Emma had thought
she'd never hear that sound again, and it added to the
feeling they'd never been apart.

"Some of the Mounties still wear full-dress uni-
forms and ride on ceremonial occasions.''

"But not you?''

His expression sobered. "I once did it all, Emma.
But to answer your question, I'm no longer Staff Sergeant Villard. Shortly before we were to get married,
I handed in my resignation to go into the family business. I wanted to be home with you every night for the
rest of our lives.''

A palpable tension stretched between them. "Tell
me about your life in the RCMP. I want to hear everything from the very beginning,'' she begged. "You
were obviously on assignment when we first met.
What were you doing in Colorado, of all places?''

Raoul shrugged and ran bronzed hands through his
hair. "It's a long story.'' He patted Fabrice's head absently. "My involvement goes back to my early twen-
ties after graduating from Queen's University in
Ontario. I'd originally thought of going into interna-
tional law, but I came to realize the work would con-
fine me too much. I needed more physical activity,
more excitement. By graduation, I'd made up my
mind to apply for the RCMP and was accepted.

"One thing led to another, and after a time I was
approached to gather intelligence for special assign-

ments. I had certain qualifications required for the job. As you know, Etienne and I spent almost every winter weekend and holiday throughout our childhood skiing at Mount Tremblant in Quebec with my uncle, a semiprofessional skier who lived in nearby St. Jovite.

"As we got older Etienne lost interest, but I often traveled to British Columbia and Alberta with my uncle, who loved mountaineering almost as much as skiing. Occasionally we rubbed shoulders with his European friends. Languages came easily to me. At times there are demands for Mounties with my particular skills. Since that kind of work appealed to me, I began accepting special cases and used my talent as a skier for a convenient cover. In fact, I turned down more than one promotion that would have put me behind a desk.

"But my family thought that was exactly the kind of job I held—an administrative position in Ottawa. For safety's sake, they never knew the truth about my work. And of course I could never tell them—especially my mother—that the ever present element of danger added a certain spice to my life I hadn't found in the comfortable, conservative atmosphere of my parents' home.

"As the years went by I spent more and more time on the move. I enjoyed the fast pace, the challenges, the excitement of living on the edge. The work made putting down roots pretty well impossible. Any relationships with women were fleeting at best and doomed from the outset.

"The nature of my assignments changed when drugs figured more frequently on the scene. When we first met, Emma, I was working in the States in a liaison capacity, gathering intelligence for an investigation concerning illegal shipments of drugs. I had my suspicions that a group of Colombians who'd supposedly been visiting relatives in Jamaica were actually flying drugs into Sorel, which is in Quebec, as well as into the Vail area."

Emma tried to assimilate everything he was saying. Little pieces of the puzzle began to fall into place faster than she could fit them.

"I'd been monitoring low-flying aircraft, which aren't detected by radar, coming in and out of the Vail area. I'd tracked a wealthy Colombian family who'd been throwing their money around and entertaining people on a lavish scale at a well-known hotel in Vail. In the midst of all this a certain female skier with impossibly long legs suddenly walked through the foyer.

"Her lovely face had a bloom of health and innocence, and her blue eyes revealed a zest for life that separated her from the people around her. When she pulled off her ski hat, all this golden hair came cascading around her shoulders like a cloud. It was you, Emma," he said huskily.

Her throat constricted. "I remember noticing you the second I walked into the lobby with my family."

"I wasn't aware of them," he confessed. "I saw only you to the exclusion of anyone else. In the space of a minute, I sensed you could become someone vitally important to me. I have no idea how I knew this, but the feelings were almost tangible."

"I know," she whispered. "I had the same experience."

"That was the beginning of the end as far as my career was concerned. I was in danger of forgetting the reason I was there. All I could think about was how I could get you into my arms. Instead of doing my job, I hung around the fireplace that night waiting for you to show up so I could ask you to dance. I suppose I needed to find out if you were a figment of my imagination."

Emma remembered it all. "I looked for you on the slopes. When you weren't there, I was afraid you'd checked out and I was frantic. That night, Dad urged me to go out to dinner with him and Lorna, but I wouldn't budge from the lodge in case I missed you."

"So the rest you know. I couldn't stay away from you, and when you left to go back to Denver with your family, I realized I'd have to do something about my situation because I wanted you in my life forever."

She stared into the flames. "After two months without a word, I decided our relationship couldn't possibly have meant anything to you."

"It meant enough that I informed Headquarters I was going to resign after I'd accomplished my objective—so I could marry you."

Her eyes closed tightly. "Were you successful?"

A triumphant smile lifted the corners of his mouth. "Between the States and Canada, we cracked the biggest drug ring ever to come out of Colombia. Several hundred people, including American and Canadian accomplices, were imprisoned. It was the most important case of my career, and I was able to leave the force knowing that what I'd done had made a difference."

She studied him intently. Because of her, his whole life had changed. "Didn't it make you want to stay in?"

"No, Emma." He spoke with such conviction she couldn't doubt him. "I craved the thought of spending the rest of my life with you and starting a family of our own. The kind of life my parents achieved suddenly seemed like heaven. I looked forward to working in the family import business and coming home to you every night. In fact, wanting to be with you caused me to make a mistake that ultimately led to my kidnapping."

Again, the dreaded word sent shivers down her spine. "What happened?" She doubted the horror of that day would ever leave her mind or heart.

"After my resignation, I took time off to be with you before returning to Canada to prepare for our wedding. What I didn't realize was that another member of the drug cartel, still in Colombia, decided to exact revenge on me and an American agent. We were their targets. They traced me back to Montreal."

"*Raoul*..."

The muscles of his body tautened. "It didn't matter that I was now a civilian. The heads of these cartels know only one thing, and they don't forgive their
enemies. They'd seen us together in Vail and kept tabs
on you, as well. They must have been spying on us
when we went for our picnic in the mountains and they
certainly knew about our forthcoming marriage. My
kidnapping was planned down to the last detail. The
miracle was they didn't kidnap you—or worse."

Emma shuddered.

"Their revenge couldn't have been sweeter, could it,
Emma?" There were tears in his voice. "When they
gagged me and stuffed me into the trunk of their car,
I knew it was all over. But I thought if God was truly
merciful, at least your life would be spared." He paced
the floor. "The nightmare of my eighteen months in
jail was wondering if you were dead, or praying to be
dead."

A hot, salty tear trickled down her cheek. "At first
I prayed to die, but not for those reasons. How did
you ever get away from them?"

"I was transferred to several jails during the course
of my imprisonment. Luckily for me, one night a fire
broke out in the compound while they were loading us
into a truck. In the confusion, the American and I escaped. He had a connection in Bogotá and we headed
there, where I managed to get in touch with one of my

former superiors. Transport was arranged and I was flown to Canada.

"Since my captors were still on the loose, it was decided I had to go underground for as long as it took to catch them, and to prevent them from tracing me or doing harm to you." His jaw hardened. "I was able to handle that as soon as I was given proof that you and our families were safe."

"You knew that?"

"When I was kidnapped, you were put under protective surveillance."

She stared at him for a long moment. All this time her movements had been monitored, while he'd been forced to exist in isolation here in the mountains. "You've lived in hell! I can't bear it."

His brow furrowed. "Let's agree we've both been there. But when I found out you were alive and well, it made the past six months at the abbey easier to endure."

The mention of the monastery brought her back to their present circumstances. "All this time you've been so close," she moaned. "What made you choose the abbey?"

"I'd spent well over a year, on and off, in these mountains and observed the priests training their dogs. It occurred to me that if I ever needed a place to hide, I could come here. I'm at home in the snow, and I've had some experience in working with dogs. So I made it my business to get to know the abbot. He became a very reliable informant. When I asked him to give me asylum, he willingly obliged and put his own life on the line."

Her heart began to pound in reaction to everything he'd told her. "How was I to know I'd find you there? Six months ago Stephen hired me to work at his clinic. Out of all the vets in the area, I can't believe we'd be the ones to service the abbey's kennel."

"When I discovered you at the kennel," Raoul said, "I thought I was hallucinating. Through my contact, I knew that you'd sold the house after your father died and that you'd qualified as a vet. But I didn't know details.

"My first thought was that my informant was working for the other side and had somehow told you where to find me as part of a plan to trap us both. When it became clear your arrival at the abbey was purely coincidental, I prayed my behavior would kill your interest and you'd go back to Denver with Dr. Channing where you'd be relatively safe."

Her eyes opened wide. "No wonder you were so cruel to me. Because of my need to find you and get answers, I forced you to risk your own safety. Forgive me." This last was barely audible, because her throat had become clogged with tears.

"Emma—" he closed the distance and sank down on the cot, gathering her in his arms "—my only concern was for *your* life," he whispered against her hot cheek. "When I saw you coming across that glacier, I knew beyond any doubt that your feelings for me hadn't changed. If anything, our separation had intensified them. *Mon Dieu,* do you have any idea how I felt?'' His lips brushed her curls. ''In trying to protect you, my silence brought you to the brink of death more than once.''

''None of that matters.'' She cradled his face in her hands. ''Now that I've found you and know the truth, nothing will ever separate us again, because I'm never letting you out of my sight. If necessary I'll stay with you in this shack until it's safe to leave. We've lost two precious years. I'm not willing to let another second go by,'' she vowed fiercely and drew him toward her, covering his mouth with her own. He followed her down and pressed her into the mattress, kissing her deeply, possessively.

She gazed at him through long, silky lashes, the blue of her eyes darkening with desire. ''Make love to me, Raoul,'' she whispered. ''I need you.''

His breath caught, and then he was kissing her with an abandon she craved. Suddenly his fingers tightened in her curls and she sensed his resistance. The next thing she knew he was pulling away from her.

''Raoul—what's wrong?'' she cried in alarm as he got to his feet.

He raked a hand through his hair. ''I can't think when I touch you, and we have to talk while there's still time.''

''What do you mean?''

''Emma, we can't stay here. You have to go back to Denver, to your life. Until these men are caught, they'll be looking for me. I'll have to keep finding places to hide out, and I have to be free in order to do that. Other lives are at stake, as well.''

"But that means another separation!'' Her head reeled at the prospect. "For how long? Weeks? Months?''

He stared at her for an interminable moment. "I can't answer that question.''

The blood pounded in her ears. "What if it takes longer?'' When he didn't say anything she searched his eyes. "You don't mean *years?*''

Clenching his fists he said, "Perhaps now you can understand why I did everything in my power to prevent this from happening. In the end, I knew that until those men were in custody, we couldn't be together.''

"No, Raoul!'' Forgetting her splinted ankle, she tried to get off the bed to reach him. But he gently forced her against the mattress, preventing her from moving.

Crouching beside her, he lifted Emma's softly rounded chin with his hand. She raised tearstained eyes and discovered moisture in his. "Don't,'' he begged. "I have to believe your coming to the abbey wasn't an accident, but a sign that one day we'll be together and nothing will ever separate us again. We have to have faith, Emma.''

Minutes passed. "I want to believe that, too,'' she said finally, fighting to keep her composure. "I love you, Raoul. There will never be another man to take your place. Never!'' Her voice broke, and she could no longer restrain her tears.

''*Mignonne*...'' He murmured the endearment against her lips and they clung with a desperation that racked them both.

''Will you get in touch with me sometimes, so I'll know you're all right?'' But he didn't answer her right away.

''The next time you hear from me, it'll be in person, and it'll mean I'm free to love you for the rest of our lives. I promise you that.'' He found her trembling mouth with his own.

Emma couldn't get enough, terrified he'd disappear from her life again before she was ready to let him go. So deep was her turmoil, she didn't hear Fabrice's loud barking until he began running back and forth between them and the door. His actions finally drew Raoul's attention away from Emma.

She could hear the drone of an engine now, and her pulse accelerated. As the sound grew closer, she realized that it came from a helicopter. Alarmed because she didn't want anything to disturb this stolen time with Raoul, she blurted, ''What do you think's going on?''

With shuttered eyes Raoul turned to her. ''I haven't had a chance to tell you yet. I keep an extra radio here at the shack in case of emergency and I called for a helicopter after you went to sleep last night. We're about to have visitors and you're about to be rescued. Put this on.'' He handed her a sweater.

Stunned by the sudden change in their situation, Emma slipped on the wool pullover and eased it down to her waist. "Why didn't you tell me what you'd done? I thought we'd at least have one more day together."

His black brows slanted downward. "You know as well as I do that to stay here for one more minute will result in our making love—and then neither of us will ever want to leave. Besides, if you became pregnant... No, for your safety, and mine, we need to get you out of here as soon as possible. This is the only way, Emma."

"Raoul—"

"I'm Father John now," he said tersely, reverting to his role so fast it left her breathless. Suddenly Raoul was the forbidding priest she'd met at the abbey kennel. Taciturn and enigmatic. "Let me make all the explanations. I'm depending on your discretion. *Tu comprends?*" When he spoke in French like that, she knew he was deadly serious.

She nodded her head mutely. There was nothing more to say, and in any event she couldn't have made herself heard. The deafening roar of the helicopter drowned out even the dog's loud barking.

Raoul opened the door and walked slowly out with a frisky Fabrice at his side. The freezing cold air rushed into the shack, and sunlight filled the entry, spilling across the floor. Its dazzling intensity blurred her vision. She'd had no idea it was so late in the morning. In fact, she'd lost all sense of time.

Within a few minutes Fabrice was back, followed by Raoul and a man wearing army fatigues and sunglasses. The two of them carried a stretcher, which they put on the floor next to the cot. Raoul stared hard at Emma while he helped her on with her parka.

"Dr. Wakefield? This is Captain Blayne. The abbey sent out a call for help. He and the pilot have been searching for you since the day before yesterday." Emma marveled at Raoul's acting ability. Even now, knowing the truth, she had difficulty remembering he wasn't a priest as he bundled the blankets securely around her, taking care not to jolt her splinted ankle.

The red-headed captain flashed her an easy smile. "That's right. We got the father's message late last night, and then the break in the weather made it easy to spot your smoke. We'll have you at a hospital within the hour and all your worries will be over."

Realizing it was expected of her, Emma whispered a thank-you, but inside she felt only a numb misery. Fabrice began whimpering soulfully, as if he perceived her feelings.

"You're lucky the father here was out training the dog. This is government property and cross-country skiers aren't allowed in the area, but you probably couldn't see the signs in the blizzard," he said as the two of them transferred Emma to the stretcher.

"The storm took me by surprise," she explained lamely, not daring to look at Raoul whose manner was remote and unapproachable. Too soon they carried her from the shack into blinding sunlight, which stung

Emma's eyes. After all this time in semidarkness, she wasn't accustomed to anything brighter than firelight.

As they placed her inside the helicopter, it took every ounce of willpower she possessed not to cry out that she wanted to stay where she was. Her hands curled into fists, her nails gouging the skin of her palms, but she didn't notice.

After strapping her down, Raoul conversed in low tones with the captain at the foot of the stretcher. "I was about to prepare Dr. Wakefield's lunch, but under the circumstances it's just as well she hasn't had anything to eat or drink in case surgery on that ankle is indicated."

"Understood." The other man nodded. "We'll have her at Denver Memorial in no time."

"Would you let the abbey know Dr. Wakefield has been picked up?" Raoul asked him. "Her colleague, Dr. Channing, will be relieved she's been found and cared for."

"Will do." The two men shook hands.

"Father?" Emma cried out compulsively, realizing her departure was imminent. Raoul glanced down at her, but no one could have guessed the intimacy they'd shared only a few minutes before.

"I want to thank you for all your help." She stared up at him imploringly, her eyes burning with unshed tears. "Some day I'd like to repay your kindness to me," she added in a desperate attempt to communicate with him. The idea that there might not be a future with Raoul was unthinkable.

"It's our life to give service, Dr. Wakefield. The reason we're here. Soon your leg will heal and you'll be able to get on with your veterinary practice. God bless you."

The sincerity of his words, a priest's words, made Emma feel as though she were part of some distorted, dreamlike reality. The scene took on a nightmarish quality when Fabrice howled mournfully and tried to board the helicopter to reach her. Raoul had to jump down and physically restrain the dog.

As the captain closed the door, she caught sight of Raoul's bearded face. For the briefest moment she glimpsed a look of anguish in his eyes. She hoped he'd seen the love in hers. The love and trust...

The rotors started up immediately, and as soon as Captain Blayne was strapped in the copilot's seat, she felt the helicopter lift off. Though she was unable to look out the window, in her mind's eye Emma could see Raoul and Fabrice receding from view. Soon they'd be mere specks in the white backdrop below, lost to her, perhaps forever. She moaned aloud at the unbearable possibility.

CHAPTER EIGHT

"YOU WON'T HAVE TO BE in this thing very long," the captain said sympathetically. He assumed obviously that she wasn't used to riding in a helicopter and attempted to allay her distress. He offered words of reassurance over and over again during the short flight to Denver.

Although Emma was grateful for his kindness, she couldn't concentrate on anything he said. She was hardly aware of reaching the hospital or being examined and questioned by nurses and doctors. All she could think about was the way it felt to have found Raoul again, to know he was alive, that he still loved her.

True to his diagnosis, the X ray revealed a simple fracture and her ankle was set in a walking cast. A thorough checkup indicated that she was in surprisingly good shape considering everything she'd been through.

The attending physician praised the expert medical care Emma had received at Raoul's hands and tried to get a smile out of her as he urged her to relax and enjoy her hospital stay. Bed rest, plenty of liquids and good food would restore her to normal health within a day or two.

But Emma was far too tense and preoccupied to take his advice. By now Raoul had probably returned the dogs to the abbey and left the area. She couldn't imagine where he'd go but knew he had contacts.

Her preoccupation with him robbed her of appetite. When her lunch tray went back to the kitchen untouched, the nurse gently scolded her, saying that she needed to eat. The nurse's words scarcely registered on Emma's consciousness. She drifted into a fitful, uneasy sleep.

"Emma?"

Her eyes flew open. "Stephen?" she muttered in complete surprise when she recognized his voice. He was standing beside the bed, still dressed in his ski clothes. Her first thought was that his presence seemed an intrusion when she'd so recently come from Raoul's arms.

Stephen leaned over the bed, his anxious eyes taking swift inventory of her drawn features and pallor. She gave an involuntary shiver at the touch of his hands. When he kissed her cold, unresponsive lips, she had to fight not to turn her head to the side. But he didn't appear to notice.

"Thank God you're alive! When Lorna and I heard you'd been rescued and flown here, we couldn't believe it. I thought I'd lost you, Emma."

The gratitude and the love in his voice filled her with shame because she couldn't share his feelings. Before things went any further, she had to tell him that because of Raoul there could be no other man in her life.

Belatedly, she noted his red-rimmed eyes and the blond stubble on his chin, which told her he hadn't slept or given himself a thought since her disappearance. The anguish still evident on his face compounded her guilt.

She moistened her lips. "I'm so sorry you've been put through all this needless trouble and worry because of my stupidity. Now that you know I'm all right, please go on down to Puerto Vallarta and enjoy your vacation."

"Without you?" he asked incredulously.

She took a deep breath. "Stephen, the experience on the mountain put my life in perspective. It made me realize I should never have come with you on this working holiday. I'm not ready for a romantic relationship with another man. In fact, I'm not sure I ever will be."

He eyed her soberly. "Because of Raoul Villard?" She nodded, averting her head. "While we were waiting for news of you, Lorna broke down and told me exactly what happened the morning of your wedding. I had no idea you'd lived through anything quite so traumatic. He must have been someone extraordinary for you to be so deeply affected."

"He was," she whispered. "I'm still in love with him and I don't see that ever changing. As long as I feel this way, I think it's best if I resign and look for another job. You're too wonderful a person to be hurt because of me."

Their eyes met for a long moment. "You won't be doing me any favors if you leave the practice, Emma. I need a vet with your qualifications. The fact that I'm in love with you has no bearing on our professional relationship. Believe it or not, I do have a life outside of Emma Wakefield. I'll survive." Despite his obvious exhaustion, he managed to give her his usual lopsided grin.

"Do you really mean that?"

"I've never lied to you, Emma. And one day I'll probably thank you for being honest with me. As far as I'm concerned, we're still partners. So hurry and get better. You're needed at the clinic." He squeezed her hand and she reciprocated, no longer carrying the intolerable burden of guilt.

"Thank you for that, Stephen."

He nodded. "Now, what can I do for you?"

"Do you know where Lorna is?"

"She and Donald followed me down from the abbey. They were waiting to talk to your doctor and told me to go see you first. I imagine they'll be walking in here any second now. In case you're worried, before I left the monastery I packed your bags. They're in Donald's car."

Emma flashed him a grateful smile. "Thank you for everything. I hope to be back at work the day after tomorrow."

He ran a playful fist beneath her chin. "Much as you're needed, don't push yourself until you're ready."

"I want to get involved again as soon as possible. I'm happiest when I'm busy." She'd have to work twenty-four hours a day to keep from thinking about Raoul.

"I understand." He gave her a swift kiss on the forehead and left the hospital room. Moments later, her older sister swept into the room, a taller, darker blond version of herself.

"Em!" Lorna hugged Emma tightly and made a place for herself on the side of the bed. For a full minute she studied her sister's pale face. "Do you have any idea what a fright you gave us? All your friends have been calling. Everybody wants to come to the hospital to see you. I told them I'd let them know if it was all right. What on earth happened to you?"

"To be honest, I don't want to see anyone else right now. Just family." Lorna had been her confidante since childhood, and they'd always told each other everything; that was part of the problem now. Emma knew she could trust Lorna, but Raoul had warned her not to tell a living soul what she'd discovered at the abbey.

But if she kept his secret, Lorna would sense something was wrong. She'd dig and dig until she had the answers she wanted. That persistence had made her a successful attorney. Emma closed her eyes, wondering how she'd ever be able to keep the truth from her.

"Em?" Lorna frowned. "The doctor says you're in remarkable condition, all things considered, so why did Stephen leave the room looking like death? Have you shut him out? The man was demented when he called to tell us you'd disappeared. Donald's outside talking to him right now. Em, don't do this," she begged. "Not now. Not when you've been making such wonderful progress. Tell me what's troubling you. Don't lock it up."

Emma couldn't bear to see the distress and alarm in Lorna's eyes, and she turned her head away. But refusing to meet her sister's steady gaze was a mistake, as Emma discovered when Lorna cupped her chin and forced her face around.

"Something happened to you up in the mountains, and I'm not talking about your broken ankle. You're acting out of character. I'm beginning to understand what Stephen meant."

Emma swallowed hard. "What did he say?"

Lorna looped a strand of hair behind her ear. "That your behavior underwent a drastic change after you arrived at the abbey."

To Emma's dismay crimson stained her cheeks, but she was saved from having to make a response by the entrance of a nurse carrying a dinner tray. With Lorna's help, she raised the head of Emma's bed and together they settled the tray on her legs.

Before leaving the room, the nurse said, "Please urge your sister to eat. She hasn't touched her food all day."

Once more Emma felt Lorna studying her and immediately started drinking the orange juice and unwrapping the soda crackers. An ominous silence filled the room, heightened by the crackling of cellophane as Emma fumbled with the package.

"You're not the same woman who left Denver a few days ago," Lorna said at last. "There's something different about you. I can feel it, and I'm warning you that I'm not leaving this room until you tell me what's wrong." Emma knew that Lorna was completely serious.

"I got lost in the snowstorm and fell into a hole. It was an experience I'd like to forget." She bit into one of the crackers and chewed deliberately.

Lorna's eyes searched hers. "No." She shook her head. "It's something else. Stephen said it started the night you were rescued by one of the priests and driven to the abbey. When I talked to Father André, he said you suffered a dizzy spell in front of the monastery and he gave you some brandy to revive you. Is that true?"

Emma swallowed the dry cracker with difficulty. "Yes. After the accident I was feeling a little lightheaded and when I started to climb out of the Jeep, I got dizzy. It was probably the combination of the high altitude and the fact that I hadn't eaten lunch that caused it."

Lines formed on Lorna's forehead. "Could you be pregnant?"

The question reminded Emma so forcibly of her conversation with Raoul she couldn't form words.

"Don't be afraid to tell me the truth," Lorna persisted with sisterly concern. "Frankly, I think it would be wonderful if you were. Why don't you have a test done?"

Emma knew how her sister reasoned and could almost hear the rest of the words hovering on Lorna's lips. If Emma was pregnant, it meant she was finally over Raoul. Much as she would have liked to use the excuse, she couldn't do that to Stephen.

"I'm not going to have a baby, Lorna. I don't feel that way about Stephen and told him as much tonight. I'll continue to work with him, but friendship is all there'll ever be between us."

Hope vanished from Lorna's eyes. "The more we talk, the more I'm convinced you're keeping something vital from me." There was a slight pause. "Did you meet someone you like more than Stephen and you've been feeling guilty about it?"

Emma almost choked finishing her juice. "How could I meet anyone? We were at a monastery!"

In a surprise move, Lorna pushed the tray aside and once more sat down next to Emma. "Tell me about the good-looking blond skier who rode the chairlift with you. Kyle something."

Emma blinked in astonishment. Until Lorna mentioned him, Emma hadn't given the man a thought. "How do you know about him?"

"Em, your disappearance made front-page head-lines and it's been the top news event on television for the past few days. There was a full-scale search and everything! It appears this Kyle was the last person to see you alive before you got lost in the blizzard. And judging by his concern, you made a real conquest there."

"But that's absurd, Lorna. He just happened to be sitting in the seat next to mine when the tour bus drove us to the lift. He asked me out for dinner, but I turned him down. He's a typical ski bum, and I'm just not interested. We rode the chair lift together, but when we reached the top of the glacier, I didn't wait for him and took off."

Lorna eyed her shrewdly. "Nevertheless, he was overjoyed when word came that you'd been found. I know he intends to look you up, so don't be surprised when he arrives on your doorstep one of these days."

"How could he do that?" Emma frowned. "He doesn't have the faintest idea where I live."

"Yes, he does, because Donald told him. The man is smitten." Lorna smiled.

"Only with himself," Emma murmured, running a hand through her freshly washed curls.

"Obviously the interest was all on his part," Lorna conjectured accurately. "Which still doesn't explain what's wrong. I was hoping I wouldn't have to ask this question, but now I'm going to. According to Father André, the priest who rescued you in the storm was a Father John who was up on the mountains training the dogs. As I understand it, he was the same priest who drove you to the abbey that first night after your car accident.''

Emma's heart was pounding so hard she was afraid Lorna could hear it. "That's right."

"Em? Did something happen when you were together? Did you find yourself attracted to him? It's obvious he rescued you in plenty of time to splint your leg and take care of you. Which means you couldn't have been out in the storm very long. Otherwise you wouldn't be in such good shape."

"What are you trying to say, Lorna?" she asked in a shaky voice, unable to meet her sister's eyes.

"Just this. You've been gone three days and nights. Anything could have happened in that period of time, and I have yet to hear you tell me a single detail of your rescue."

"I lost my sense of direction in the storm and fell into a crevasse. It was the dog, Fabrice, who found me and alerted the priest." Emma hoped that telling at least part of the truth, as much as she could safely divulge, would satisfy Lorna. "He—the priest—risked his life lowering himself down to splint my leg and carry me to safety."

"And where was that?"

"A cave."

"So you survived three days in a cave without heat or food?"

"It wasn't a cave exactly. When he works with the dogs up on the mountain, the priest lives in a stone hut. There's a fireplace and provisions, camping equipment."

"I thought as much," Lorna murmured after a prolonged silence. "And you'd just broken your ankle, which means he had to nurse you. You're a beautiful woman, Em. Given the right set of circumstances, any man would be tempted by you—maybe even a priest. Did something happen between the time he took you to safety and the arrival of the helicopter? Did he take advantage of you?"

"For heaven's sake, Lorna. I had a broken ankle!"

"Since when did that stop nature from taking its course? You've always been a terrible liar because you're so transparent. Look me in the eye and tell me nothing went on."

"Stop sounding like a prosecuting attorney!"

"I only sound that way because you feel guilty about something. Em, don't you know I love you and that I want to help? Stephen rode down to the accident site with this priest when they rescued you the first night, and he told me Father John is one of the younger monks. It all fits."

"And from *that* you've deduced something went on?" Emma exploded, feeling herself break down bit by bit under Lorna's barrage of questions.

"No," Lorna said gently, smoothing the curls at Emma's temple. "It's something else. There's a light in your eyes again, Emma. A kind of...of glow. Raoul once put that light there, but it went out when he disappeared. Now it's back."

Lorna had always been intuitive, but right now her powers of observation were uncanny. Emma felt herself weakening. If she didn't tell Lorna the truth soon, she'd fall apart. And it would be such sweet relief to share this....

"You can deny it all you want, but I know my sister inside and out. Is it possible that within three days you grew attached to the man who saved your life? Are you upset because he's a priest? Have you done something that's made you feel guilty?"

"Oh, Lorna!" Emma's cry came out on a muffled sob and she dissolved into tears.

"Tell me what's wrong, honey."

The minute Lorna's arms went around her, the words started tumbling from Emma's lips. "Raoul's alive, Lorna, impersonating a priest. As soon as he saw me he ran away, but I found out where he was hiding and skied across the glacier to find him."

"*What?*" Lorna gasped, gripping Emma's shoulders so she could really look at her.

"Shh..." Emma whispered, and put a finger to Lorna's lips. "You can't tell another soul, not even Donald. Swear it!" she demanded with an intensity that seemed to shock her sister.

Lorna nodded frantically. "I swear it, Em. Raoul's really alive? It's so hard to take in."

"I couldn't believe it, either." Her voice trembled. "Not at first. He has a full beard and mustache now."

For a quiet moment they simply gazed at each other, as Lorna clutched both of Emma's hands. Then she took a deep breath. "I need answers to a thousand questions, Em, but I guess there's only one that really matters. Why did he disappear on the morning of your wedding day?"

Emotion welled up inside Emma until she couldn't breathe. "He—"

"Emma Wakefield!" Donald called out as he strode into her room, preventing further conversation. "If you ever do this to us again, I swear my heart won't be able to stand the stress." He kissed her on the lips, hugging her and Lorna at the same time.

Emma was crazy about Lorna's husband, a warm, fun-loving man with a genius for the stock market. He'd been like a protective older brother to Emma from the moment he and Lorna had started going out together.

"I don't plan to repeat the experience, believe me," Emma said brightly, flashing him a smile meant to cover a multitude of sins.

"Thank heavens for that." He grinned and pinched her cheek. "You're still a raving beauty, even with your peg leg. Did Lorna tell you we're taking you home with us to recuperate when you're released?"

"I love you for saying that, but it won't be necessary. I plan to go back to work the day after tomorrow. All I need is a good night's sleep."

"She does," Lorna jumped in. "In fact I was helping her get ready for bed when you came in. Right now she should have some rest. Why don't you watch television in the waiting room until I come out?"

"Did you hear that, Emma?" His eyebrows shot up wickedly. "Sounds like she's trying to get rid of me."

"I am, so scoot!"

Donald glanced at Emma, then his wife. "I smell a conspiracy here. Whatever you two were whispering about when I came in has me totally intrigued. If I do as you say, then tomorrow I expect to hear the unexpurgated version of your experience, just like Lorna. After all, we're related. Is that a deal?" He swooped down and kissed the end of Emma's nose.

"It's a deal." She made a sound between a laugh and a groan and reached up to hug him again. Lorna was a lucky woman. "Don, thank you for being so wonderful. I'm sorry my accident upset everyone and took you away from your work."

His wry expression had her laughing. "Normally I love any excuse that gives me time off. Not this time, though. But now that I know the outcome, I can enjoy the rest of the weekend. Sleep well, Emma. We'll see you in the morning—at which time I expect to hear every fascinating detail of your ordeal."

After kissing his wife, he left the room. Emma watched as Lorna put a Do Not Disturb sign on the outside of the door.

"All right," she whispered, easing herself onto the mattress and clasping Emma's hands again. "Tell me everything from the beginning. Don't leave anything out."

Emma discovered how desperately she needed to talk about Raoul, as she poured everything out—from the first encounter with "Father John" to her departure in the helicopter. Lorna sat spellbound and didn't say anything until Emma ended with, "I'll wait for him no matter how long it takes."

Lorna shook her head. "Who would have dreamed he was a Mountie, of all things? But honey, you've got to face the fact that you might never see him again. He's a wanted man as far as the Colombians are concerned and they'll stop at nothing to find him and—"

"Don't say that!"

Lorna put her hands on Emma's shoulders. "You have to face reality. If you hadn't seen him at the abbey, chances are you'd never have known what happened to him. That's why he tried to elude you and wouldn't make love to you. He's done the honorable thing in letting you go. He knows his chances of survival are poor at best. Don't you see? You'd be an utter fool to let hope of a future with him destroy your life!"

Emma lifted a ravaged face. "You don't understand. He believes we're going to have that life. He told me to have faith, and I promised him I'd wait."

"For how many years? Em, he never expected to see you again! He's lived a life people only read about in books, and it started a long time ago. Like he said, there's a great deal more at stake than just the two of you. He can't make any guarantees."

"Why are you being so cruel?" Emma's eyes were swimming in tears.

"Because I saw what his disappearance did to you the first time around. I don't ever want to see you go through that again."

She grabbed Lorna's arm. "I know everything, now, so this is entirely different."

"Is it? You're still waiting and hoping for something that may or may not come to pass. If anything, matters are worse than before because now you have expectations. Honey—" she smoothed the damp tendrils from Emma's hot forehead "—I realize that finding him has been as traumatic as losing him. But he's gone again, and you could easily waste the rest of your life waiting for an event that'll never take place."

Emma didn't want to listen to any more. "It's my life, Lorna," she said bitterly "but I'll make sure I don't burden you and Don."

"Oh, Em." Lorna reached for her and hugged her hard. "I love you so much. Forgive me for playing the big sister. I should have my tongue cut out. Go on hoping and dreaming, honey. Maybe one day a miracle will happen and you'll be together. I do have eyes in my head—I can see there's only one Raoul Villard. He's got to be the world's greatest heartbreaker. Trust my little sister to be the woman who eliminated all the competition."

Emma unbent enough to laugh with Lorna between the sobs and tears.

"If the nurse walked in right now, she'd blame me for upsetting you and she'd have good reason." Lorna sniffed and plucked some tissues from the box on

Emma's night table. "I know you're exhausted, so I'm going to let you sleep. But I'll be back first thing in the morning and we'll have breakfast together. If you need to talk during the night, promise you'll call me."

Emma clung to her hand. "You won't tell Don?"

"Em. I'm an attorney. I know very well the slightest leak could put Raoul—all of us—in grave danger. I've given you my word. To everyone in the world but my little sister, Raoul Villard is dead." She bent down and kissed Emma's cheek. "Sweet dreams. I'm sure you've stored enough memories over the last three days to keep you going for a long time."

Emma's eyes blazed a hot blue. "Until he comes for me."

Lorna patted her shoulder before leaving the room. As soon as she'd gone, the nurse came back to check Emma's vital signs and give her a mild sedative. To her own amazement, she slept through the night and didn't wake up until the doctor made his rounds the next morning.

He pronounced her well enough to go home after breakfast, as long as there was someone to wait on her for a few days while she got used to crutches. Donald and Lorna arrived as he was leaving the room and arrangements were made to release Emma from the hospital. After eating, Lorna helped her dress while Donald went to collect a wheelchair and a pair of crutches.

Shortly afterward, the nurse unexpectedly poked her head in the door. "You have a visitor, Dr. Wakefield. Shall I tell him to come in?"

Emma wanted to say no, but gave the nurse a reluctant nod. She didn't feel like talking to anyone and was glad to be going home before she was deluged with well-wishers. "It's probably Stephen," she murmured to Lorna from her chair beside the bed. But it was Kyle Rawlings, the blond man from the ski bus.

"Hello there." He breezed into the room, winking at Emma before flicking his gaze to Lorna. "I had to come and see how the patient was doing. From what I can see, she's doing terrific!"

Lorna flashed Emma an I-told-you-so look. But Emma wasn't the least bit happy to see him. His cocky attitude repelled her. She frowned when Lorna said, "I'll be right outside."

Kyle's light blue eyes glinted with male admiration as Emma quickly adjusted the hem of her skirt over her knees.

"Except for a broken ankle, I'm fine, thank you. In fact, I'm on my way home right now."

"That's good news. I was afraid you might never be found in that blizzard."

"I'm sorry so many people were inconvenienced."

"Sorry enough to have dinner with me one night soon? I found out you're not engaged or anything, and that really made my day. Naturally I wanted to find out how you managed to get away from me while my back was turned." His eyes twinkled, as though to let her know he'd forgiven her.

He had the all-American good looks one associated with athletes. In fact she imagined, he was a real hit with college-age snow bunnies, particularly because he was probably close to thirty and had a practiced charm. But she liked him even less on second meeting. Not only was he too aggressive and presumptuous, he was typical of many athletes who assumed they were irresistible to the female of the species.

"I was anxious to ski a run before the storm began. In my haste, I obviously took a wrong turn and became disoriented."

"Well, weren't you lucky that priest was able to find you so quick and take care of you."

"Actually it was the dogs who found me. Otherwise I would've died." Emma was unwilling to tell him more.

"I don't even want to think about that. How about going out with me this weekend? I'll give you a call."

"I'm afraid not. You see, I'm in love with someone else. He's the only man in my life," she said with a tremor in her voice.

Kyle didn't look quite so confident now. "Is it the vet you were with at the abbey?"

"Yes," Emma lied baldly. More than ever she didn't like this man's audacity.

"Your brother-in-law seemed to think I stood a chance."

Emma's anger grew white-hot. "If I'd been interested in you, I'd probably have skied with you."

"Well," he sighed, "you can't blame a man for trying. I'll call you sometime, in case you change your mind."

Her facial muscles tautened. "The answer will still be the same. Now if you'll excuse me, my family's waiting to take me home."

CHAPTER NINE

EMMA'S APARTMENT in a modern Denver complex was only five minutes from the veterinary clinic. After her father's death and the sale of the family home, it suited her to move into a small place of her own that held no memories.

Part of its appeal stemmed from the fact that she could walk to work. But all that had changed since she'd broken her ankle. After eight long weeks, the doctor had finally removed the cast and pronounced Emma fit. Still, to be on the safe side particularly since the streets were icy with midwinter chill, Lorna insisted on driving her to and from the clinic for another few days.

"Good night," the receptionist said, poking her head around the door of Emma's office. "Stephen's already gone home, so I guess you're the only one left."

Emma looked up from some medical records she was filling out. "Good night, Kitty. Have a wonderful time with Paul. I'll close up here. Lorna won't be coming by for another ten minutes."

A terrible envy stole over Emma when the receptionist had put on her coat and left. Emma normally schooled her thoughts about Raoul, especially during working hours. But Kitty's happiness with her fiancé reminded her of everything she was missing—and might never experience again. She couldn't always control her fears and lately her black moods seemed to be increasing.

Emma crushed the phone message from Kyle Rawlings, which was on her desk. He didn't understand the word "no." Since those days in the mountains, she thought of Raoul with every phone call, every piece of mail, every ring of the doorbell. Even driving with Lorna and Don, she'd looked for his face in every car, every crowd. This insanity had to stop!

Disturbed by her state of mind, she threw on her coat, locked the office and went outside, still hesitant to put her full weight on the injured ankle.

As soon as she got in the car a few minutes later Lorna said, "We've got tickets to the symphony tonight. I bought an extra one for you. Why don't you come with us?"

Emma's first impulse was to refuse Lorna's invitation. The soul-stirring music of Brahms and Tchaikovsky would bring Raoul too vividly to mind and deepen her depression. On the other hand, she'd made a promise to herself to get on with living in spite of the pain.

"That sounds wonderful. Thank you."

Lorna darted her a knowing glance. "I realize it's the last thing you want to do, but I'm glad you're not shutting yourself off from life. I'm proud of you, Em."

"You shouldn't have said that," Emma whispered as tears coursed down her cheeks. "I'm not handling this at all well. I try to keep a smiling face around my friends and the people at work. But you were right when you told me the waiting could end up destroying me."

"I'd suggest you go away on a vacation, but I know you'll never leave Denver now."

Emma stared out the window with unseeing eyes. "I couldn't bear it if he came while I was gone."

"Well, one night at the symphony won't put you out of touch for very long," Lorna said quietly as the car pulled up in front of Emma's apartment building. "Don and I'll be by to pick you up at seven."

"Thanks, Lorna." She squeezed her sister's arm before stepping out of the car. A snowfall the previous night had turned the sidewalks to ice. Having no desire to spend the next two months in another cast, Emma made her way carefully into the building.

She'd barely taken off her coat when there was a knock at the door. It was probably her neighbor Phoebe, but with one part of her mind, she always expected to see Raoul.

She gasped when she discovered who was standing in the hall. *"Etienne!"* The shock of seeing Raoul's older brother rendered her speechless.

"Emma..." He gave her a smile reminiscent of Raoul's and reached for her. They hugged for a long

time before he kissed her on both cheeks and entered
the apartment. Emma's heart thudded sickeningly in
her chest. Had Raoul made contact with his family at
last? Was that why Etienne had flown all the way from
Montreal?

"Come in and sit down. Let me take your coat.
How's your mother?" She hadn't phoned Madeleine
Villard in almost four months. And since finding
Raoul, Emma didn't know how she could talk to her
again—at least, not until he resurfaced. It would take
a better actress than Emma to pretend she didn't know
Raoul was alive. Guilt over her secret consumed her.

"Not well, I'm afraid."

Emma bit her lip. "I'm so sorry. Can I get you tea
or coffee? It's such a cold night."

He shook his head but remained standing, adding
strength to Emma's conviction that his visit had to do
with Raoul. "Nothing for me." His dark, somber eyes
held hers for a brief moment. "Emma, I have something to tell you. *Maman* and I talked it over and felt
you should hear it in person."

A band seemed to tighten around her chest. "I-it's
about Raoul, isn't it?" Her voice shook, and she could
hardly breathe.

"*Oui.* I think you'd better sit down." He guided her
gently to the couch and sat beside her.

Sickness rose in her throat as she stared at him
helplessly.

"Three days ago *Maman* received word that Raoul's
body had been found."

It took a moment for Emma to comprehend the words. When she finally did, her whole body froze. *"What did you say?"*

He grasped her lifeless hands in his own. "I know how you feel," he murmured compassionately. "The family's in shock. It doesn't seem possible after the years of wondering and waiting for word of him. Any word..." His voice faded to a tearful whisper.

White-faced, Emma broke free of his grip and got to her feet. "I can't believe it, Etienne. Who called Madeleine? How do you know it was really Raoul?"

Slowly he stood up, his complexion ashen. "Because I was given his personal belongings and there can be no doubt."

"Dear God!" Emma's cry resounded in the apartment. As the world began to reel, Etienne caught her around the waist and eased her back to the couch. She held on to the lapel of his suit jacket. "Wh-who found his body? Where?"

He bowed his head. "Emma, first you need to know that since his disappearance, Raoul has been living with the monks at the Abbey of the Holy Cross, not far from Vail where you both loved to ski. Do you know of it?"

Did she know of it? Emma buried her face in her hands as her shoulders shook convulsively. Etienne held her in his arms and rocked her.

"Apparently Raoul went missing, and one of the abbey's dogs who was devoted to him finally found his body buried in an avalanche not far from the monastery. He'd been dead about six weeks. The abbot reported it to the police and they phoned *Maman.* I flew out immediately to speak to him. We had a long talk. It seems that two years ago Raoul had been struggling with a problem none of us knew anything about. In desperation, he'd gone there to work it out and decided to become a priest. A fine one, from all accounts."

Emma was aware of Etienne's voice, but she felt disembodied and couldn't respond. *Raoul had been murdered!* And it was because of her! If she hadn't pursued him so relentlessly he'd still be safe at the monastery.

She wanted to die and must have said the words aloud because Etienne began shaking her.

"Emma!" he pleaded in a frantic voice. "*Mon Dieu,* don't talk that way." Just then he sounded so much like Raoul she could hardly bear it. "Painful as it is to face, the nightmare's finally over."

Emma groaned in agony. Neither Etienne nor the Villard family had the slightest conception of what had gone on in the mountains when she'd traveled there with Stephen. For them, the news of Raoul's death had to be a bittersweet blessing, one that would bring relief after more than two years of soul-destroying speculation and conjecture.

For Emma, hell had opened its jaws.

"I've just come from the abbey where they held their own services for Raoul. They've buried him in their graveyard. Now I'm on my way home to Montreal. We're going to hold a memorial service for him there at the family plot. Roger's seeing about the marker. Come with me. *Maman* needs you right now. So does Roger. You'll always be part of our family." His loving words caused Emma to collapse in his arms.

"When they found him, he was wearing his watch, the one Papa gave him before he died. It survived the avalanche and I want you to have it." He pressed something into her hand.

In a stupor, she lifted her head to gaze through the tears at the familiar watch with the round face and Roman numerals. She remembered Raoul wearing it, looking at it, during their time together. The tangible evidence before her eyes made his death a reality she could no longer deny.

"Raoul..." She cried his name aloud as her hand closed tightly over the precious keepsake. She clutched it to her breast. "Thank you," she whispered between sobs.

Etienne wept with her. "I know he would've wanted you to have it. In spite of what he did, he loved you, Emma. If it's any consolation, you're the only woman he ever cared about and he could've had his pick. Women swarmed around my brother, but he never seemed to notice them. Then he met you. According to him, it was love at first sight."

Emma kissed Etienne's wet cheek. "He loved you, too. His fondest memories were of the two of you skiing at Mont Tremblant with your uncle. He adored you and Roger," she whispered with heartfelt emotion. It would be so easy to tell Etienne the truth, but since the abbot had chosen to keep Raoul's past life a secret, Emma could do no differently. Raoul had sacrificed his life to eradicate a great evil in the world. She would sacrifice something, too, and honor his memory by remaining silent.

"Will you come?" Etienne asked again in a tone of pleading as he wiped his eyes with a handkerchief.

"Yes. I want to come." Struggling to get her emotions under some semblance of control, she pulled out of his arms and got to her feet. "Excuse me. I need to be alone. Please make yourself comfortable and help yourself to anything you need." Etienne nodded in understanding.

Still holding the watch, she walked on rubbery legs to her bedroom, where she could indulge her grief in private. When she finally emerged, she discovered Lorna and Donald in the living room, deep in conversation with Etienne. She'd forgotten they were coming by to take her to the symphony.

Emma met Lorna's tear-filled gaze, then she flew into her sister's arms. "Etienne's explained everything," Lorna said softly. "We're flying to Canada with you. Tonight. I'll pack your bags." Numbly, Emma nodded, unable to think, let alone function.

As before, she scarcely remembered the last-minute preparations, including the conversation with Stephen or the subsequent flight to Montreal. All that really stood out in her mind was the great bonding she felt between the families as they surrounded the marker. Emma was still too dazed to really hear the prayer offered by the pastor—the same priest who was to have performed the marriage ceremony.

As a frail, arthritic Madeleine stooped to put flowers at the base of the marker, Emma knelt on the mat with her and together they placed the sweet-smelling yellow roses next to the other flowers, a final tribute to the brother, son and man they all loved.

Snow fell around them. Montreal glittered with winter beauty, Raoul's favorite kind of setting. Even the elements seemed to be paying homage to his memory, yet all she could think about was Raoul's murdered body finally laid to rest in the abbey's cemetery.

For Emma, the end had come. Now she had to live the rest of her life without him. When she rose to her feet, she knew she must get away from ice and snow, from memories, or there'd be no point in going on....

"COME ON, PRINCE. Time to go back."

The Great Dane tugged on his leash, not eager to return to his pen at the clinic's boarding kennel.

"Prince," Emma commanded in a stern voice, planting her bare feet in the sand so the undertow wouldn't sweep them into the ocean. The surf was up along the San Juan Capistrano coastline, a location that had appealed to her from the beginning. In the five weeks she'd lived in Southern California, she'd started to acquire a tan and had become fairly adept

at body surfing. In time she hoped to master the surf-
board.

At the job interview, Flossie Hardy, owner of the
veterinary clinic, had taken an instant liking to Emma,
who spent the day observing the older woman's tech-
niques and clientele.

Emma, in turn, felt a genuine affinity for the veterinarian who'd lost her husband a year earlier. The
intelligent, dynamic woman was a true dog-lover like
Emma, but was getting on in years and found she
couldn't handle the practice alone. Thus the need for
an assistant.

At the end of the day, Flossie offered Emma the
position. Emma accepted on the spot, a decision she'd
never regretted. The clinic-cum-boarding kennel was
situated on the beach side of the highway. It included
a tiny but charming rooftop apartment—Emma's new
home—with a living room that overlooked the ocean.
Flossie lived in the beach house next door. This was a
perfect arrangement as far as Emma was concerned,
offering both convenience and privacy.

Flossie Hardy led an interesting life of her own and
didn't pry into Emma's personal affairs. As a result,
the two became fast friends and devised their sched-
ules so that Emma worked mornings and Flossie af-
ternoons, though Emma was generally available to
help out if Flossie's shift was busier than usual. Eve-
nings and Sundays they took turns being on call.

Emma had always enjoyed mornings. She liked
getting up early to feed and exercise their boarders

before business hours. Not ready to have a pet of her own, she adopted the whole kennel and felt a particular fondness for Prince. The dog paced his stride to stay beside her as they ran along the beach toward the kennel, making a game of avoiding the big waves that crashed against the shore. A glance at Raoul's watch told her it was already eight-thirty, and the clinic opened at nine.

She loved the salt spray and the sound of the pounding surf. Best of all, there was nothing about the ocean that had associations with her past. Naturally she missed Lorna and Don and her friends, especially Stephen. But she found a kind of comfort, almost a pleasure, in her new surroundings and routines. Besides, her family—and Raoul's—were only as far away as the telephone if she felt in the mood to talk.

Here in San Juan Capistrano, she was making friends with neighbors and clients who knew nothing about her former life. Several men she'd met on the beach, as well as at the clinic, had asked her out. So far she hadn't accepted any invitations because she didn't feel ready for a relationship, even one as uncomplicated and casual as an evening at the movies.

Maybe in time someone she could care about would come into her life, but she doubted it. For now, her career was enough and she devoted all her energies to it. Flossie worried that she was working too hard, but Emma didn't mind the extra hours. Taking care of animals provided a constant source of satisfaction and gave her a reason to get up in the morning. Beyond that, she didn't expect anything else of life.

Raoul lived in her heart. Alone at night, she fell asleep with poignant memories of their times together. When remembering became too painful, she turned on the light and read from the latest veterinary journal. Eventually her eyes would close and the magazine would fall to the floor....

A tug on the leash brought Emma back to the present. Giving Prince's ears an affectionate rub, she put him in his pen and dashed upstairs to her apartment to change into a skirt and blouse and grab a bite of breakfast before work. It never failed to amaze her how full the reception room was on the dot of nine.

She was kept so busy she didn't realize Flossie had already come in for the two-to-six shift and was dealing with a client on the phone. Emma had just treated a Pomeranian who'd eaten a box of chocolates and gone into convulsions. After telling the hysterical owner the dog would have to be hospitalized overnight until its condition was stable, Emma went out to join Flossie at the desk.

When she told the older woman what had happened, Flossie shook her head ruefully. "One of these days I'm going to write a book that'll rival James Herriot's," she muttered.

"I believe you could." Emma grinned. "There are as many unusual characters living here as in Darrowby."

Flossie nodded and adjusted her glasses. "Say, I know you're off now, but before you go anywhere, I wondered if you'd make a house call. I've just been talking with Mrs. Hilliard, the woman who brought in her Irish terrier for his shots last week."

"I remember," Emma said, jotting down notes in the last patient's file. "Did he have a bad reaction?"

"No. She's calling for a sick tenant whose dog has the heaves. Apparently they're without transportation. I promised I'd drop in for a look, but I think the dog should be seen right away. Do you mind?"

"Heavens, no. I'll buy lunch on the way. What's the address?"

"That's the tricky part. It's at the other end of town, on the second street that winds to the right off Point Loma. It looks like a private drive because there's no sign, but it's Tavish Road. She lives at number three. Call on her first and she'll let you into the apartment upstairs."

Emma hung her lab coat on the peg and grabbed her purse and satchel. "I'll find it. See you later."

"Be careful as you go." Flossie always said that when Emma went anywhere.

Reversing her small convertible out of the garage, Emma joined the string of cars headed south on the coastal highway. Though overcast, the spring day was balmy and the warm breeze tousled her curls, which were much longer now that she'd been growing out her hair.

Hungrier than usual, she pulled into a roadside restaurant a few minutes later and ordered a chicken fajita and a ginger ale. Once she'd eaten, she headed for Tavish Road.

If Flossie hadn't given her specific directions, Emma would've been lost. After living in a methodically laid-out city like Denver all her life, she found these neighborhoods confusing. But she located the address easily enough, a two-story cedar frame house perched on a steep slope amid a veritable jungle of flowering red oleander. Emma got out of the car and with satchel in hand climbed the tall, narrow stairway. She could hear a dog barking long before she reached the top.

A middle-aged woman with platinum-blond hair stepped outside, the terrier at her heels. "Oh!" she said in surprise when she saw Emma. "I was expecting Dr. Hardy. I met you last week, didn't I? You're..."

Emma extended her hand. "I'm Dr. Wakefield, her associate. I hope you don't mind that I came in her place." She leaned over and patted the dog's head. "I see he's his frisky self again."

"Oh, yes. Cleo has more energy than I do. Thank you for getting here so quickly."

"I understand you called about a sick dog."

"That's right. Mr. Carlisle doesn't have a phone and has been ill himself. Walk around the side of the house and you'll see a staircase leading to the apartment. I've left the door unlocked for you. However, the last time I checked, the dog was lying on the porch. Apparently he's been heaving.''

"I'll attend to him," Emma assured the woman and hurried toward the stairs, anxious to make the dog comfortable as quickly as possible.

She wasn't prepared for the sight that greeted her. At first glance, the magnificent Saint Bernard lying on the porch at the head of the stairs looked as if he were dead. If he'd been heaving before, there was no sign of it now.

The more she looked at him, the more he reminded her of the short-haired Saint Bernards bred at the abbey in Colorado. That recognition brought a wave of memories that made the tears spring to her eyes.

Opening her bag, Emma pulled out her stethoscope and sank to her knees to examine him. The minute her hands touched his fur, the dog began to moan and he lifted his large head. He stared at her with his solemn, dark eyes.

Emma froze. It couldn't possibly be... But how many dogs had that distinctive mask? "Fabrice?" she whispered incredulously.

He barked and inched toward her, plopping his head down on her thighs, swishing his tail back and forth.

"It *is* you!" she gasped in stunned surprise. She hugged him around the neck while he wriggled delightedly and licked her hands and face. He was obviously as overjoyed to see her as she was to see him.

But her joy quickly changed to unmitigated fear when she realized what was really happening here.

Raoul's killers had traced her to California and were using Fabrice as bait.

He wasn't sick! This was an elaborate setup and the woman downstairs had lured Emma to the scene—like the proverbial lamb to the slaughter. Her body broke out in a cold sweat.

As her fingers tightened in Fabrice's fur, she recognized that this was the beginning of the end. Amazingly enough, Emma felt the panic subside and a strange sense of inevitability take its place. Before she became the next victim, she wanted, needed, to confront the man responsible for Raoul's death.

Slowly she got up from her knees and, with Fabrice at her heels, walked over to the partially open door. The fear had fled. All she could summon was an intense anger that had been building for more than two years—an anger now focused on something and someone tangible.

She knocked determinedly on the door. "Mr. Carlisle?" she called in a clear, steady voice. "It's Dr. Wakefield. I know who you really are. Why don't you come out in the open and face me before you kill me like you did Raoul Villard? Or are you too much of a coward?"

When there was no response, a white-hot rage consumed her. "I'm coming in." The anger gave strength to her limbs as she walked through the doorway to an empty living room.

She turned to the dog at her side. "Where's he hiding, Fabrice? Take me to him!"

CHAPTER TEN

"I'M RIGHT BEHIND YOU, *mignonne,* and can assure you I have nothing more on my mind than making love to you for the rest of our lives."

For a moment the world stood still.

She felt as if she'd been trapped between two dimensions.

"I told you to have faith because one day I'd be free, and I'd come for you in person. That day is here, Emma."

After believing him dead, she found the familiar sound of his deep, rich voice so startling she didn't immediately grasp the meaning of his words. Then, in a pure revelation, it came to her that Raoul's death and funeral had been part of a master plan. Otherwise he wouldn't be here. The details didn't matter. She spun around, her brilliant blue eyes ablaze with light.

Except for the shorts and T-shirt, he looked exactly as he had the first time she'd caught sight of him at the lodge in Vail. He was clean-shaven and deeply tanned. His black eyes shone with love out of an impossibly handsome face, and Emma's heart turned completely over.

"Raoul!"

With an exultant cry, he swept her into his arms and swung her around, crushing her tender mouth beneath his. Emma couldn't get close enough as they kissed long and hard and passionately, over and over again, trying without success to appease the fierce hunger that had built up during the cruel years of separation.

"I can't believe this is happening," she whispered deliriously against his lips, relishing their taste and texture, feeling the lines and angles of his beloved face with her hands.

"*This* is all that kept me alive in that jail, all that kept me sane on the mountain. Hold me, Emma, love me!" His voice trembled. He caressed her with wild abandon, molding her to the hard length of his body, convincing her he was truly alive and safe in her arms at last.

"How I've waited and longed and prayed for this day." He buried his face in her neck, kissing the pulse throbbing there.

Intoxicated by his touch, she moaned, but Raoul's mouth stifled the sound, and his kiss transported her to a world where only the two of them existed, where their only thought was to please each other.

Eventually they made their way to the couch, their bodies entwined. "I love you," they both murmured at the same time. Smiling that even their thoughts were so perfectly attuned, they touched each other's faces in wonder.

Tears ran down his cheeks, telling Emma what this moment meant to him. Unbearably moved, she leaned over him and began pressing tender kisses to his mouth, his chin, his nose, his brow, her salty tears mingling with his.

"What happened to you after I was flown out? I nearly lost my mind with worry."

He cupped her face in his hands. "That shack was my bolt hole in case of trouble. I'd made several trips there with the dogs throughout the summer, planting emergency stores and a radio. Fabrice knew where to find me, but I have no doubts he could've tracked me there even if the terrain had been entirely unfamiliar to him.

"In any event, when I radioed the abbey, one helicopter was sent for you and another came for me."

"Is that why you didn't make love to me? Because you knew we didn't have time?"

"That was one of the reasons," he admitted, nibbling her lower lip sensuously. "But you did have a broken ankle, my darling, which seems to be perfectly healed now, thank heaven. I was terrified that if I started making love to you, all thoughts for your welfare would go out of my head. Most of all, however, I didn't want to leave you with a child you might have to raise on your own."

"I wish you had," she said emotionally as more tears escaped. "I don't think you have any idea how much I love you. Having your baby would have meant everything to me." Suddenly words weren't enough, and she drew his mouth close to hers. For long minutes, they forgot everything else in the joy of discovering each other all over again.

"I have so many questions to ask," she murmured against his smooth-shaven jaw. Somehow his other, bearded persona had been more forbidding and inaccessible. The Raoul who cradled her in his arms now was the same man who'd lain in a meadow with her high up on a mountainside one glorious fall day and whispered his love.

Raoul found her mouth and kissed her until they were both shaking with need before he asked, "Where do you want me to start? It's impossible to think, let alone talk when I'm holding you like this, kissing you..."

A mischievous smile lighted her face. "Try, for my sake, but don't move. Not one inch," she begged and brushed her lips enticingly against his.

But her lightheartedness quickly changed to tears as she burrowed her face against his throat. She breathed in the familiar tang of the soap he used. "I have a problem, my love. You've known all along you were alive, but I'm still trying to believe it. In fact, I can't believe I'm holding you like this again...that you're actually here."

He laughed quietly and nuzzled her ear. "I'm very much here and feeling more alive than I've ever felt before," he said huskily before covering her mouth with his once more.

Fabrice chose that moment to thrust his head between them. His low, moaning sounds made it clear that he didn't like being ignored.

Just as Raoul's body began to shake with laughter, uncontrollable giggles bubbled out of Emma. Soon they were both breathless and gasping. Raoul's uninhibited laughter was the most glorious sound she'd ever heard.

After patting Fabrice who barked from sheer happiness and swished his tail back and forth, Raoul told him to lie down again. The dog gazed soulfully at Emma, hoping for a reprieve, but when there was none, reluctantly complied with Raoul's command and lay back down on the floor next to the couch.

"Rule number one, Emma. Our bedroom is off-limits to him," Raoul whispered in her ear, wrapping her tightly in his arms once more. She nestled even closer and murmured her assent. His mouth was doing the most marvelous things and she never wanted him to stop. "And speaking of our bedroom, I want to marry you right away, but the ceremony will have to take place behind closed doors."

Emma shifted a little in his arms and eyed him anxiously. "You're not still in danger, are you?"

His expression sobered, reminding her of that other Raoul. The lines that suddenly marred his handsome face made him look years older. "I'm afraid we'll have to be careful for a couple of years until the danger is past. Do you think you can live with that?" She heard actual fear in his voice and was astounded by his vulnerability where she was concerned.

She slowly lowered her head and kissed the palms of his hands before placing them against her heart. "You can ask me that after everything we've been through?"

Her answer brought a glow to his face. "We eliminated the men who were after me. But inevitably
there's someone else sent to replace them. That's the
way they work." He smoothed the gold tendrils away
from her temple. "With any luck, my death and buri-
al have put them off the scent for good, but we'll take
extra precautions for a while longer, just to be sure."

Shuddering, Emma moved closer. "I have to hear
what happened to you after I left in the helicopter—
everything! You couldn't know what a helpless feeling it was to be plucked from your arms like... like a
rabbit in an eagle's claws, while you and Fabrice were
left behind to face who knew what."

Tremors shook Raoul's powerful body as he clasped
her tighter. "My heart was in that helicopter with you,
Emma. Talk about a helpless feeling."

"Where did you go, darling?"

"Fabrice was flown back to the abbey, and another
priest was sent up to the hut to take over training the
dogs. I was flown to Denver to meet with my co-
workers. While I was there, the person assigned to
keep an eye on you notified us of your unexpected
hospital visitor. It was the one important break we'd
been waiting for. From then on, everything went like
clockwork. More surveillance was set up until we
could close in."

Completely confused, Emma turned in his arms so
she could look at him. "Who are you talking about?
What visitor?"

"Kyle Rawlings."

She shook her head. "What does he have to do with anything?"

"He works for the Colombians and uses skiing as a cover. That's how I found out about him in the first place, but we'd never been able to pin anything on him until now."

"I can't believe it!" Emma gasped quietly. "How long had he been following me?" The idea made her feel sick to her stomach.

"When I escaped from jail they were watching you night and day, holed up in a building across the street from yours in the hope I'd turn up at your apartment."

Wordlessly she threw her arms around his neck and clung to him as his words sank in. "That means he trailed Stephen and me to the abbey. He knew my every move. Raoul, I practically led him straight to you without realizing it!"

He kissed her into silence. "The beauty of it all is that you eluded him, something he hadn't anticipated. And that made him angry. So angry, in fact, that he took the risk of exposing himself by showing up at the hospital."

Through gritted teeth she said, "I thought he was one of those awful, overgrown, womanizing ski bums who hang around ski resorts picking up unsuspecting females. I couldn't stand him on sight. When he showed up in my hospital room, I was ready to have him thrown out."

"Fortunately for me, you didn't," he teased. "Our man followed him back to his apartment, where he met with the Colombian who'd kidnapped me. The Americans were able to keep tabs on both of them from then on. It didn't take long before they were caught with the goods and arrested."

"Thank God," she whispered.

Raoul's lips tightened. "Did he ever do anything to you, Emma? Did he ever touch you?" The possessive tone of his voice sent delicious chills through her body.

"No. But he was far too aggressive and insisted on riding the chair lift with me even though I let him know I wasn't interested. When we arrived at the top and he bent over to adjust his bindings, I skied away. My mind was on you. All I could think about was getting across that glacier to you."

"Your disappearance obviously looked contrived to him, particularly when three days later you were found at the hospital in relatively good condition."

"It's all beginning to make sense. For a total stranger, he was way too friendly with Lorna and Donald."

"He's the dregs of society, Emma. They all are. But it's over now. As soon as I was debriefed, I made contact with the abbot. He was a willing participant in planning my 'death.' I owe him everything, Emma."

"I'd love to meet him and thank him for being so wonderful to you."

He drew her body against him, and she could feel the beating of his heart. "I'd like him to marry us."

"I want that, too, but what about your family? Do they even know you're alive? They love you so much and—"

"I've already had my reunion with *Maman* and my brothers. Stop looking so anxious, *mignonne.*"

Emma didn't realize she'd been holding her breath. Her eyes closed in relief. "They must have been ecstatic."

"At first I was afraid *Maman* might have a coronary from the shock, but she seemed to recover quickly. As for Roger, he's in love as usual, but it's still nothing serious, and Etienne and Marie are working on their third baby. Everything considered, the family's doing remarkably well. They're all eager to help us plan another wedding at the house. This time in secret, with only family members present."

"Could we have two ceremonies? One in Montreal for the families, and another in the mountains just for us?" She gazed up at him, her eyes full of love. Then she smiled, almost shyly. "I can't wait to tell Donald and Lorna."

Raoul smiled back. "Why don't you pick up the phone and we'll break the news together? I've missed your family and want to thank them for taking such wonderful care of you while I've been away."

She caressed his face, tracing the strong, defined shape of his cheekbones, his chin. "Before we do that, I want to know how long you've been in San Juan Capistrano."

"Two weeks." Emma groaned. "I had to wait that long to establish myself and let things die down. I've been getting friendly with my landlady so she'd help me reunite with my girlfriend. She was only too happy to oblige." He followed the curve of her lips with his finger. "You made all the right moves. Coming to California was inspired."

She swallowed hard. "I had to do something if I was going to survive the rest of my life without you."

"You're the most courageous woman I've ever known, Emma. In fact, I almost had it in my heart to feel sorry for the man you thought was hiding in here waiting to do his worst to you. Without hesitation, you charged in here like an avenging angel. Your performance was every bit as magnificent as that trek across the glacier."

"I had incentive, my love. It was my only way to you." She gave him the benefit of a full-bodied smile. "How did you get Fabrice to play dead like that?" At the mention of his name, the dog lifted his head expectantly. Emma scratched his ears affectionately and he licked her hand before dropping his head back onto his paws.

Raoul chuckled softly. "Have you forgotten he and I spent a lot of time together up on that mountain? Teaching him tricks helped keep my sanity during those long, lonely hours. The abbot gave him to me— and to you—as a gift. A wedding gift, he said. Wise man."

She tried to smile but suddenly burst into tears again. "You'll never know what that memorial service was like."

His sharp intake of breath told her so much. "All of this has been hell for me, too, darling. But it was the only effective way to end the nightmare. Unfortunately we still have a difficult problem ahead of us."

Emma's heart fell to her feet. "What do you mean?"

A sweet, quizzical smile broke out on his face. "Do you think you can put up with being married to a man who has no job and comes to you with nothing more than a loyal dog in his possession? A man who has to keep a low profile for at least a few years? One who'll be constantly underfoot and wants nothing more than to make love to his beautiful wife whenever he can get his hands on her?"

Emma smiled through the tears. "The real question is, does he have the stamina to be loved by Emma Wakefield? A woman who's been waiting for over two years to start her honeymoon? Are you sure he's up to it?" Her eyes danced.

"*Mignonne,* it's obvious there are many things you have yet to learn about me."

"I've been trying to, believe me."

His smile faded, to be replaced by a more serious expression. "I own a house on a wooded hillside in the Laurentians. I've always considered it one of the most beautiful spots on earth to raise a family. The nearest town's a few miles away, and we wouldn't be that far from my family.

"We could live there in relative peace and quiet. We'll work on your French. Then, when you pass the qualifying exams to practice in Quebec, you could set up a clinic. Donald and Lorna could come for visits and ski with us. Do you think Dr. Hardy will mind very much if I whisk you away from here today? I want you to be my wife before I take you to bed for the first time, and that moment can't come soon enough for me."

Emma could scarcely find words. "When I tell her our story, she'll beg us to leave, with her blessing. Raoul—" she searched his beautiful dark eyes "—could we go to the hut after we say our vows at the abbey? It's spring now. I can't imagine a more perfect place to begin our life together."

MORNING SUNLIGHT filtered through the stained-glass window of the abbey chapel, illuminating Emma's wedding dress, in shades of blue and rose. For the second time in two days, she stood next to her husband, who wore a dark gray silk suit with a gardenia in the lapel as he'd done the day before in front of their families. She couldn't take her eyes off him.

Raoul winked, sending her a private message of love before the abbot pronounced the words that made them husband and wife. From the moment she'd entered the chapel and caught sight of Raoul, she'd been too bemused to pay much attention to what was going on. Father André and Father Gregory were their only witnesses, yet she hardly remembered shaking their hands as they beamed at her and offered their blessings.

Emma was so happy she didn't think she could contain her emotions much longer without bursting. "Father," she addressed the abbot, "and all of you—" her voice caught as she turned to the other priests "—thank you for helping Raoul, for... for saving his life."

She felt Raoul's arm slide around her waist and then he, too, smiled at the abbot. "Amen to that," he said quietly. "Emma and I also want to thank you for letting us use the hut."

The kind old abbot nodded graciously. "It will always be there for you."

An hour later, after a private wedding breakfast in the refectory, they changed into their climbing gear. Raoul grasped Emma's hand and they started for the hut. They wore no packs because everything had been prepared for them and sent to the hut ahead of time. Fabrice took the lead.

The combination of the high altitude and Emma's growing excitement made her heart beat rapidly. The color rushed to her cheeks as she contemplated the moment when they'd be alone again, out of the world's sight, and able to express their love freely and fully. Last night Raoul had made her his wife in every sense of the word, but the hours had flown by far too quickly. . . .

Every little while Raoul sent her a message of such frank longing she feared her legs wouldn't support her. "Am I real to you now, *mignonne?*"

Emma paused before taking another step. "So real I can't get to the hut fast enough," she admitted as more hot color filled her cheeks.

"Neither can I," he said fiercely, and before she knew what was happening, he'd picked her up and put her over his shoulder in a fireman's lift. "We'll make better time this way."

"No, darling. You'll hurt your back!"

"We're almost there, Emma."

They were. She could see the huge outcropping of rocks concealing the stone hut straight ahead.

Despite the snow, the air was definitely warmer. Signs of early spring were all around them. Emma delighted in the hearty pink and yellow primroses pushing up through the rocks to reach the sun.

Fabrice romped in the snow and chased after everything that moved. He, too, was obviously experiencing the euphoria of being back home again.

When they finally arrived at the hut, Emma felt as if they were standing on top of the world. Raoul put her down gently, then wrapped his arms around her from behind and hugged her close. Together they gazed out over layer upon layer of snowy mountain peaks, spreading in every direction as far as the eye could see. For Emma, the grandeur of the Rockies had never been more in evidence.

"How could I have thought I hated winter?" she asked in wonder, leaning back against his solid male warmth.

"I hated it more than you did," he whispered against her neck, caressing the warm skin with his lips. "Until a miracle happened and my brave, beautiful wife defied death to come to me in my darkest hour."

His words affected Emma profoundly. She blinked back tears, staring across the vast expanse of the glacier with its thousands of hidden fissures and crevasses. There were no clouds today. This was the first time she'd actually been able to see it in all its pristine, terrifying splendor. "I actually crossed *that?*" she whispered.

A shudder passed through Raoul's body as he buried his face in her fragrant, golden hair. "You, and only you." He turned her in his arms. "No man ever had greater proof of a woman's love." He kissed her forehead, then her lips—lightly, almost reverently. "Now it's my turn to show you what you really mean to me. Let's go inside, Emma."

Her limbs seemed to melt from the adoring look in his eyes. Once more she found herself being carried through over the threshold of the hut.

A certain Saint Bernard gazed wistfully at the two humans he worshiped before they disappeared, shutting the door behind them. With uncanny perception, he understood they needed to be alone.

Recognizing that it would be a long time before he was summoned, Fabrice trotted back to his vigil on the rocks, where he passed the time watching the clouds soar through the intense blue Colorado sky. It was a wonderful day!

HARLEQUIN
Romance

A Christmas tradition...

Imagine spending Christmas in New
Orleans with a blind stranger and his aged
guide dog—when you're supposed to be
there on your honeymoon!
#3163 Every Kind of Heaven
by Bethany Campbell

Imagine spending Christmas with a man
you once "married"—in a mock ceremony
at the age of eight!
#3166 The Forgetful Bride
by Debbie Macomber

*Available in December 1991, wherever
Harlequin books are sold.*

RXM